SEVERED

AN EXTREME PSYCHOLOGICAL HORROR
STORY

WARREN BARNS
THE BARNS BROTHERS

Cover art by Warren Barns

ISBN-13: 978-1974459575

Published by Broken Barn Publishing

For my sweet angel, whose innocent eyes will never read the words on these pages. You make me a better man.

CHAPTER 1

Seth drifted in and out of consciousness, from blissful sleep to growing awareness of the space around him. It wasn't like his usual morning hangover after a night of hard drinking and partying. He felt great, spaced out and happy, though a bit uncomfortable lying in the bathtub. The waist deep water must have been ice cold because he was numb from the hips down, but he was so comfortably serene he didn't care at all. His eyes rolled around in their sockets, and he found it hard to focus on his surroundings.

At first, he thought he was in his bathroom back home, but he laughed at his own stupidity. They didn't have a tub in their shitty little apartment, only a shower. It could mean one of two things; either he ended up crashing at someone's house and the bathtub was the only available resting place, or he hooked up with another nameless chick, came home with her, and fell asleep in her bathtub to avoid the post coital awkwardness in her bedroom. Neither scenario was a stretch. Both had happened before. With a warm blanket, a bathtub could be the most comfortable bed in the house. But he wasn't wrapped in a blanket, and the ice cold water was biting at his numb skin.

Seth blinked and tried to focus his drifting gaze at his outstretched hands in front of him. He noticed something attached to his arm, but his vision was blurry and he couldn't see clearly. He pulled at the small piece of pink plastic, which popped out of his skin. A trickle of blood flowed from the puncture wound in his arm.

"Mother fucker!" he cursed as he held onto his bleeding arm.

The water surrounding him up to his waist was brown, with small blocks of partially melted ice cubes floating around in it. Everything stank of iodine, and his skin was stained orangey brown.

Why the fuck do I have an IV line in my arm? And why am I in a bathtub full of freezing water? And why is it brown? Did I shit myself?

He pushed himself up out of the water and something pulled in his groin. The pain was somewhere between a kick in the nuts and a terrible muscle spasm. In other words, worse than childbirth. An instant wave of nausea washed over him and he projectile vomited across the length of the bathtub covering his chest and abdomen in spew.

His groin ached even more as his abdominal muscles contracted to expel the acid contents of his stomach.

He squinted his eyes to see better. Slowly, the room around him came into focus.

He looked about the bathroom and had no idea where he was. He'd seen the inside of a lot of girl's bathrooms, but this one was foreign to him. In fact, it looked more like the kind of bathroom you'd find in a cheap motel.

A cold shiver ran up his spine. He had to get out of the freezing, murky water before he got hypothermia.

This is the worst fucking practical joke ever. I bet it was Mikey who did this. I'm gonna fucking kill him when I see him.

Seth rested his hands on the sides of the tub and pulled himself up to his feet. He let out a deep grunt as a spasm hit him right between the legs so hard he doubled over.

He lifted a leg to climb out and his foot caught on the metal chain connected to the plug. Seth fell against the edge of the bath and slipped, landing with a thud on the hard linoleum floor. He twisted his back and hit his head hard. The brownish water in the bathtub swirled and went down the drain with a loud whooshing gurgle.

"Fuck me, that hurt," he said, rubbing the lump that was growing on the back of his head.

The pain in his back and head subsided, but still he had the ongoing gnaw in his groin. Seth reached down to massage out the ache. As his hand went between his legs, he pulled back in shock and horror.

"Holy shit!"

He patted himself down in disbelief.

"My cock! My balls!"

There was nothing between his legs except for a neat row of oozy stitches running from his pubic bone down to his taint. His cock. His balls. His big sack. It was all gone.

Seth whimpered and shook. He laughed and then he cried.

This can't be happening. I'm dreaming. Who the fuck would do this to me?

He flattened out his pubic hair and bent over to see better how badly disfigured he was.

Seth covered his eyes and prayed, but when he opened them, his penis was still gone. His whole body trembled in anger and fear. Seth turned toward the mirror and stared at his reflection. It took more than a moment for him to appreciate the full horror of what was reflected in front of him. His prize possession. His favorite toy. His family jewels had been stripped from his body by some cruel monster.

My penis! Where the fuck is my penis?

"Help!" he cried. "Somebody help me!"

There was a loud knock on a nearby door.

"Hey, open up!" shouted an angry male voice from somewhere beyond the bathroom walls.

"Help me," screamed Seth. "Please call an ambulance."

"Call an ambulance? It's half past ten," the angry man continued shouting at the front door. "You're supposed to be checked out by nine. If you're not out in ten minutes, I'm calling the police."

What if he's the one who did this to me? He has to be. But I don't remember a thing from last night.

The door was locked. At least whoever was out there couldn't get in.

Then it must have been me who locked the door. But I don't remember. There's no fucking way I'm opening the door and letting that guy in.

A crisp breeze blew through the room, chilling him to his bones. Seth ran to the window that was an inch ajar, pushed it open and looked out. He was in a room on the second floor of a run down motel. The pool in the concrete courtyard below was green tinged, bottles and beer can debris bobbing on the surface. Junk was strewn everywhere from what must have been a ripper of a party the night before. There was an emergency stairwell right outside the window, and fresh brown scuff marks on the ledge.

There was a loud bang on the door. "Hurry the fuck up. And why the fuck do you need an ambulance?"

Seth knew it was bound to be fruitless, but he quickly searched every inch of the bathroom floor, the trash can, and the shelves in the desperate hope that maybe his junk was somewhere nearby.

They can attach it again, right? They can do face

transplants. They'll be able to reattach my dick and balls, right?

The closest he came to finding his missing appendage was an old discarded condom lying in the dirt behind the bath.

"Shit."

He ran cold water in the basin and rinsed his face, a part of him still clinging to the hope that this was a bad dream, that he would wake up if he washed all the sleep from his eyes.

Seth felt a trickle running down his left leg. He looked down to see a tiny stream of blood flowing from the gash between his legs. Acid wash rose in his mouth and he clutched onto the hand basin, trying to hold back the vomit.

When the wave of nausea had passed, he started rifling through the drawers below the basin until he found what he was looking for, a packet of sanitary pads. There were only two left. The writing on the side of the packaging promised to provide *"The best absorption for ladies with a heavy flow"*.

Emasculated and deflated, Seth extracted a pad and held it in the air. He examined it from every angle, struggling to figure out which way the wings were meant to be aligned to follow the natural contours of *down there*.

He grabbed the nearest towel hanging on a rail beside the bathtub. It was cold and damp and a stale smell filled the air as he lifted it off the rail. He wiped the blood off his leg and tossed the towel aside.

Seth thought back to some of his earliest memories as a child, of seeing his mom put her sanitary pad into her panties, before pulling them up and adjusting the fit. It was the one thing he always thought was disgusting about girls. Nothing made him soft quicker than a girl who was on the rag. What could be more disgusting than sticking his dick into a bleeding orifice? It was a cruel joke that once a month his happy place would become a monstrous thing of nightmares.

He'd fucked a chick once who'd neglected to tell him it was her time of the month. He was happily banging her doggy style when he looked down and saw blood all over his dick. He thought he'd hurt her, or worse, himself. He'd been rough, as always, the way they liked it, but not enough to rip off his foreskin. He'd even used lube that time because she whined about him being so much bigger than her last boyfriend. Yet somehow there was lube mixed with bright red blood all over his dick, and starting to dribble down onto his balls.

Seth abruptly stopped thrusting and excused himself from the bedroom. He ran to the bathroom, grabbed the shower head and blasted his privates to wash them down. After examining his dick from every angle, he was sufficiently reassured that he was still intact. But that could only mean that he'd left the girl — whose name he couldn't remember — bleeding to death in the bedroom.

He raced back to the bedroom, expecting to find

her pale corpse lying in a pool of blood pouring from her broken vagina. Instead, she was lying on her back, fingering herself with one hand, and squeezing her tits with the other. She was gasping for air as she climaxed, hardly taking notice of Seth watching from the doorway.

"Oh, oh, oh, oh my goooooood," she squealed with delight.

He stood in the doorway, mildly queasy, unable to take his stare away from the girl's blood tinged fingertips. She scrunched up her face and scowled at him.

"Why are you standing in the door? And what the fuck happened to you? I was enjoying that. I was so close to coming and you just left."

"I saw blood, and..."

She rolled her eyes to the heavens.

"You guys are all the same. It's a pussy, Seth. Do I need to remind you what it's made for?"

She wiped her fingers on the sheets and climbed out of bed.

Her body was totally smoking. She had girly abs, a perfect ass, and a brand new set of fake tits that her daddy bought her for her 18th birthday. Seth felt himself stiffen as she pressed her body against his.

"I don't think *he*," she glanced down at his hard cock wedged between their abdomens, "has a problem with me having my period."

He wrapped his muscular arms around her tiny frame and cupped her ass cheeks in his large hands. Seth delicately ran his nose across her forehead, down her neck, inhaling her sweet natural perfume. He planted tiny kisses on her neck and nibbled her ear.

"How about I fuck you in the ass?" he whispered.

Her body stiffened.

"Whoa," she said, putting a hand on his chest and pushing him a foot backward. "You what?" she said incredulously.

Seth shrugged and gave her a lopsided grin. The same smile that had melted the hearts of many a lustful girl before this one.

"Let me get this straight?" she said, almost laughing as she spoke. "You think it's disgusting to fuck my tight little pussy a couple of days a month when it's going through a perfectly natural process." She paused and shook her head. "But you don't have any problem with sticking your dick where the sun don't shine, and covering it with my shit and millions upon millions of infection causing bacteria?"

She was right, it sounded disgusting, too. He was thoroughly convinced not to do her bareback.

Seth jumped in. "Don't stress, babe. We can use a condom."

She poked his chest hard with her index finger, over and over again, pushing him down the hallway.

"No, Seth, *we* are not doing anything, any more. I don't want to waste my time with a little *boy* who got his sex education from porn, who tries to make me feel bad about myself for being a woman. I am not a fucking sex doll."

His back pressed against the cold wooden frame of the front door at the end of the hallway. The girl reached past him and turned the handle, pulling the door into his back.

"Get the fuck out of my house, you fucking loser."

She shoved him out the door, stark naked. He tripped on the door ledge and swung his arms madly in the air to catch his balance. It was 3 o'clock in the dead of night, and no one was around to see him do the walk of shame, sneaking down the apartment stairwell and outside to the street where he'd parked his car.

Seth wished he'd got that girl's number, or name. She clearly needed a man who could challenge her, but she'd taken him by surprise. He admitted that he could have done better in the moment, but nobody is perfect.

He wondered what she would think of him right now. Would she be laughing her ass off, or would she give a damn? He pictured her face as she stood over him, cackling like a witch, and pointing at him, trying to attract the attention of anyone who cared to look at the pathetic display of a former man lying on the ground at her feet.

Seth ran his hand over the smooth mound where his dick and balls used to be and sobbed. With every passing minute the dull ache in his groin throbbed harder.

CHAPTER 2

14 Hours Earlier

Seth was so excited he was starting to sweat. Everything was perfect. Half a dozen red roses were sitting beside a chilled bottle of *brut* champagne and box of Belgian chocolates. He'd sacrificed the other half dozen roses for their petals, which were sprinkled across the slightly yellowed bed sheets.

After turning the main lights off and throwing a pillowcase over the bedside lamp shades, he'd achieved the perfect level of mood lighting to hide all the room's imperfections. He'd read a story once about how duvet covers in motels never get changed, that if you shined a black light you'd find evidence of every kind of bodily secretion soaked between the fibers. Needless to say, the duvet was tucked under the bed where it would never come in contact with Seth's naked skin.

If only he could have done something about the group of college kids next door who were already drunk and partying hard. He plugged his iPhone into his portable Beats speaker and started playing Ed Sheeran loud enough to drown out the dance party next door.

This girl wasn't like the college girls he'd indulged in since leaving high school. She was mature. A woman. Only twenty-eight years old but she may as well have been from a completely different generation compared with a carefree young guy like Seth who still lived under his parents' roof and by their rules. She was a legal secretary with a penchant for muscled young studs and handcuffs... or so her profile said. Seth had stopped reading once he got to the pictures.

Her name was Lucy. She'd been the one who made contact first. Girls weren't usually that forward, but who could say no to a rack like the one she'd sent him to drool all over — the female equivalent of a dick pic.

But where was she? She told him to be there by 8:30 p.m. He'd arrived ten minutes early to find the motel room door unlocked and no one inside.

Lucy had left him a cupcake sitting in front of the TV and a handwritten note that read "*Eat Me*".

An Alice in Wonderland reference? She's a classy gal. Why the hell not?

She'd also left her lacy underwear draped over the

bed in preparation for later. Seth salivated over the tiny thong and giant bra cups. He flipped over the note and saw there was more written on the underside.

I'm sorry, Seth. I got all the way here and realized I'd forgotten to feed my cat. Back in twenty minutes. So so sorry. Make yourself comfortable.

— Lucy xox

The girl's gone home to feed her pussy. Just like I'll be doing all night long.

He chuckled as he munched on the cupcake. Red velvet with chocolate ganache. His favorite.

So that's why she asked what my favorite cake was!

There was a bitter aftertaste that complemented the sugary sweetness. Best red velvet cupcake he'd ever eaten, didn't want to waste a single crumb.

Seth rinsed the sticky icing off his hands in the bathroom hand basin. He stared at his reflection in the mirror, ran his fingers across his designer stubble and cocked one eyebrow.

Sexy bastard, if I say so myself.

He adjusted the uncomfortable swelling in his pants. Being somewhat *larger* than the average guy had its disadvantages when it came to wearing stylish, yet comfortable clothing. A burden he carried with pride.

He'd even gone as far as trimming his pubes and the smattering of hair on his chest for this hookup. Made sure he'd cleaned especially well under his foreskin, and knocked one out in the shower so there was no risk of arriving prematurely during the opening act. Didn't want to leave anything to chance. Not with a hot piece of ass like Lucy who would have high expectations.

Why am I so tired? It's not even nine o'clock yet.

Seth yawned.

"Shit, I might have to crack open the champagne early."

He blinked his tired eyes and tried to maintain focus, but his eyeballs kept turning inward, cross-eyed, his vision going double.

Seth went back through to the bedroom and sat down on the edge of the bed. His head hung heavy on his shoulders.

Why am I so...

His head hit the sheets and the rose petals bounced and settled on the bed around him.

He stared up at the ceiling, the room spinning in circles above him.

The door opened and someone entered the room. A shadow was cast over Seth.

"Lucy?" said Seth. But he didn't have the energy to lift himself up to see who was there.

Why am I... so... tired?

CHAPTER 3

Present Day

Arriving at the motel and eating the cupcake. That was all he remembered.

Seth had a sudden, desperate urge to take a dump. When it didn't pass after a couple of seconds he realized it had to come out, right there and then. He sat down on the toilet and his guts growled at him. Seth pushed and a squirt of liquid came out his asshole, followed by the most intense pain he'd ever experienced in his entire life. His shit might as well have been made from razor blades. It hurt so bad he stopped pushing halfway through the log — big mistake — the intense agony of his sphincter bearing down brought tears to his eyes. He pushed again, through the tearing pain and dropped the kids off at the pool. After the agonizing cramps subsided, his body felt as if it were floating.

Seth grabbed a wad of toilet paper and wiped. Something definitely didn't feel right down there. He looked at the toilet paper which was slick with clear lube and flecks of blood.

What the fuck did she do to me? Was it even a she?

He couldn't recall actually seeing who entered the motel room. It could have been anyone. Any freak with access to pictures of a hot girl.

How could I be so stupid?

He'd been tricked by a pervert, a predator with an internet connection. His suspects were now narrowed down to literally millions of sick bastards around the country.

Seth flushed the toilet and tried to forget about it, didn't want to even consider the possibility that he'd been violated in his unconscious state.

When he looked around the bathroom again, he saw something he hadn't noticed before. In the corner, beside the toilet, on top of a heap of old magazines, was a pile of clothes. *His* clothes. And sitting on top of them was a mobile phone. His underwear was neatly folded beneath the phone. He placed the sanitary pad between his legs and put on his boxer briefs. Then he picked up the phone, one of those cheap smartphones that nervous parents gave to their kids to call home if they were ever in trouble, or the kind cheaters used to text their lovers and send dirty pictures behind their partner's back.

It was fully charged and there was a notification on the screen.

"1 new message"

His index finger trembled as it hovered and finally tapped the grubby screen. The message opened.

— *Hi Seth. Text me back when ur awake xox*

Seth's breathing quickened as a thermonuclear rage built inside him. He clenched his fist into a tight ball, unleashed an unholy roar of fury, and punched the wall.

Oh my god, so much pain.

Despite the powerful analgesics floating through his bloodstream, he was still aware of the bones in his hand crunching and splintering from the force of the blow. He clutched his hand and wept in pure agony.

He'd done a real number on his hand. The knuckles were bleeding, skin split and raw. His whole hand throbbed.

You fucking idiot, Seth. Don't you ever fucking think before doing anything? That was so fucking stupid.

He ran his hand under cold water. Slowly, the pain faded to a dull ache. He didn't blame himself for what he'd done. It was perfectly reasonable to lose his shit at a time like this. Who wouldn't want to punch something if they woke up to find their dick and balls severed from their body, and what looked like a message left behind by a well meaning psycho stalker?

He was afraid to use anything in the bathroom to wrap around his hand, in case he caused himself a raging infection from whatever flesh eating bacteria lay hiding in wait for him. He'd been careless when he wiped the blood off his legs. Not again. His shirt would have to do. He picked it up and looked at the cartoon text on the front that read — "BIG" with a large picture of a rooster beside it.

He wrapped the shirt around his hand, wincing with each rotation of the fabric around his battered paw. Seth gathered his jeans and put them on. There was a grey hoodie at the bottom of the pile, which didn't belong to him. When he opened the neatly folded hoodie, he recognized his college athletics team logo immediately.

Fucking stalker! A chick did this! Some fucking stalker psycho bitch with a crush.

He was assuming it was a girl who'd done this to him. He'd had gay guys hit on him in the past, for whatever reason, but they wouldn't have cut off his dick and balls to teach him a lesson. Would they? This was the kind of thing only a chick off her psych meds would be capable of doing.

He put on the hoodie — a perfect fit — and

picked up the phone again. He read the message twenty times, growing angrier and angrier every time. He knew he had to stop and try to think straight.

But his fingers had other intentions. He bashed out a reply to the text.

U fuck! What did u do to me? —

He sent the text before his brain had a chance to catch up and stop him.

"*Sent*"

"Shit!" he muttered. "Shit, shit shit," he called out over and over again.

The phone started tweeting like a tiny bird — *Tweet tweet, tweet tweet.*

Seth looked at the screen.

"*1 new message*"

He tapped on the message.

— :-(

Oh what? Now I hurt your feelings?

Seth laughed. He couldn't believe what was happening.

Tweet tweet, tweet tweet

He looked down at the phone.

"1 new message"

He tapped the message, less hopeful than last time that he'd get a meaningful response.

— *Don't worry. I forgive u.*

Think, Seth, think.

I'm sorry —

He sent the message and waited, his heart nearly pounding its way out of his heaving chest.

— Don't worry. Ur precious bits are safe. U'll get them back if u follow these simple instructions.

Tell me what I have to do. —

— I'll call u

The phone began to ring — *"Ring, ring, ring, ring, bananaphone"* — in a shrill chipmunk voice.

"555-0135 calling"

She was holding all the strings, wasn't she? He realized he was doing it again, assuming it was a chick. It had to be.

He answered the call.

"Hello?" said Seth.

"Hello, Seth," said a deep, modulated voice.

She, he, it, who the fuck cares, they know my name. How the fuck do they know my name?

The same intense rage began to build inside him again. He wanted to scream every insult that ever was, reach down the phone line and rip out the throat of whoever was talking on the other side.

"What do you want from me?"

"I only want the best for you, Seth."

The voice went quiet.

Seth was tired of the games already, but what choice did he have but to play along with it.

"What have you done with my... with my..."

He couldn't bring himself to say it out loud.

"Your cock? It's okay to say the word, Seth. It's not a dirty word. It's also the name of a common farm animal. It's what you attribute it to that makes it bad."

Seth seethed and gritted his teeth.

"Don't worry," the modulated voice continued, "I knew what I was doing. I followed the YouTube video instructions to the letter." The voice giggled.

Seth was right. It was a chick. No amount of voice modulation could disguise that naughty schoolgirl giggle.

"All your bits and pieces are on ice. You've got about 36 hours until it's too late for them to be reat-tached. If you want to be reunited with your favorite toy again, you've got to follow these simple rules.

First: do not tell anyone about what has happened to you, not the cops, not a doctor, not your best friend, no one. Second: you have exactly twenty-four hours to complete the three tasks that I have set out for you to redeem yourself. Third: there is a bottle of pills on the shelf. Take a blue one every four hours, and a white one every six hours. They're painkillers and antibiotics. If you miss a dose, you'll probably get sepsis and die. And we wouldn't want that happening."

Seth gripped the phone tighter in his trembling hand.

"If you don't follow these three simple rules, I will dispose of your junk, first the balls, and then your penis, into the waste disposal. I don't want to do this. I want you to be whole again."

He didn't know what to say, afraid that if he opened his mouth a torrent of abuse would be unleashed that would seal his fate, and the fate of his private parts forever.

"Take the first pill now, Seth."

He put the phone down and scanned the shelves for the bottle of pills. There they were, right in front of the mirror above the handbasin. The bottle even had his name printed on the side. He took a closer look at the dispensing label. The pills came from a drugstore near the university campus. He'd been there once before to get a morning after-pill that he slipped into an ex girlfriend's coffee after a night of unprotected fun. He usually chuckled when he thought back to her complaining about how bitter the coffee was that he'd brought her in bed the next morning. Even earned himself some morning head. Usually. But not today.

Seth tipped out a blue and a white pill, just as the voice had instructed, and swallowed them without water. The dry tablets caught in his throat and made him gag. He quickly turned on the cold water and scooped up a handful to wash down the bitter pills. He tipped out the contents of the bottle in his hand. There were enough pills to last exactly twenty-four hours.

"Seth, you there?" said the modulated voice over the phone.

He lifted it to his ear.

"I've taken the pills," he said coldly.

"Good boy," the voice replied.

I'm not a fucking dog, you bitch.

He came so close to saying his thoughts out loud.

"Do you remember what happened three years ago?"

Seth stood on the spot in stunned silence.

"February 14th ring any bells?" she asked. Still, he stood there stupefied. "Valentine's Day?"

He trawled through his memories. The last couple of years had been a blur of non stop alcohol fueled partying. One day had blurred into the next, and it was a miracle he passed his exams. Well, most of them. Although he was suspicious that his father, who was on the Board of Trustees, had something to do with it.

His dad had sat him down and had a stern talk about "his direction in life" after he got let off with a warning from campus security for driving home drunk from a party. But his dad was an asshole who expected him to be just as intellectual and dedicated to his career as he had been. Seth just wasn't the same kind of man as his father. His father was a dweeb who played chess and thought tennis was a team sport. Seth was more like his mom, whose closest thing to a career was running the weekly Women's tennis club morning tea and round robin tournament.

Nope. Nothing came to mind.

"Oh, Seth, I'm disappointed." The voice sighed. "Let me remind you then. You were at an infamous frat party. The one where Kerry Jones supposedly gave up her virginity to the entire football team. Remember now?"

Seth's throat tightened as if a ghost were squeezing and trying to wring the life from it.

"What about it?" he said, his voice breaking.

"You don't have to lie to me, Seth. I'm here to help you find redemption."

Seth felt faint. He put the phone down on the shelf in front of him and pushed the loudspeaker button. He gripped the hand basin while the room started spinning around him. He dry retched, nothing left in his empty stomach to up chuck.

"You do remember," said the voice.

"Of course I fucking remember," he snapped.

And instantly he regretted it.

There was silence from the phone, and after a few seconds the call ended.

Seth grabbed the phone. "No, no, no, no, please don't hang up," he called out.

How could he forget Kerry Jones, the pretty church-going freshman from across state who became a national embarrassment for the University when a video was released online of her supposedly losing her virginity to every guy on the football team during one night of frat house debauchery? At least that's what the title of the video inferred. The identities of the guys involved were never revealed, but the video featured a fair number of young men in letterman jackets, and so the connection was made. Somehow, the cameraman avoided capturing any of their faces, and the heavily edited action focused solely on Miss Jones and her doll eyes as she took them in every orifice for hours. Kerry stole the crown that slutty Debbie from Dallas had worn for decades.

She claimed it was rape, but she had no one to charge, no memory of what happened at the Valentine's Day frat house party that she'd been invited to, along with half the campus. There was DNA evidence, lots of it, but no one to tie it to. No policeman believed her story. No judge would preside over a case without a perpetrator. No one knew if it actually was the guys from the football team who'd slept with her. That was just the title of the video — "Slutty virgin pops her cherry with every guy on the football team". It got renamed a few times during its fifteen minutes of Internet infamy, but the gist was always the same. No one stepped forward to tell the truth. Whoever the guys were, none of them owned up to being on the video.

Kerry's father told the press that she'd been drugged and those boys forced her to perform disgusting sex acts that she would never have consented to had she been sober. And most people would have believed him, but the scandal made for such great news that everyone was talking about it, and like starving wild animals they devoured every salacious detail as more emerged.

When her parents found Kerry dead in her bedroom with a bloodied pair of scissors, and a deep gash through the carotid artery in her neck, there was silence from the media. The fun was over, and no one dared to speak of the events any more. The press that had been camped outside the Jones' house dispersed, and people made themselves forget, lest they have to share in the responsibility of an innocent young girl taking her life because it was no longer worth living.

As if Kerry Jones' parents hadn't been punished enough, their younger daughter, Julie, had a psychotic episode and ended up in the funny farm. She couldn't cope with the invasion of privacy and constant school-yard bullying and taunting. Apparently they had a family history of schizophrenia. Something about stressful life events being triggers for those kinds of things to reveal themselves. Nobody knew what happened to Julie after that. Nobody really cared.

Seth leaned against the wall and started to slump down to the floor, but the stretch of stitches in his groin stopped his descent. He stood bolt upright again from the shooting pain and stared around the room.

I need to get the fuck out of here. I'll go straight to the cops. Someone who knows me is responsible. The police will be able to find who did this to me. It'll be alright. It's all going to be okay.

He almost had himself convinced.

Then phone rang again.

"555-0135 calling"

He tried to ignore it. What good was going to come from helping this psycho fulfill their sick agenda? He should stop now and resign himself to the fact that his life would never be the same again.

But life without his dick? Was *that* even a life worth living?

He answered the call.

"You were rude to me, Seth. Please don't do that again. I stood beside the kitchen sink for almost a minute with one of your testicles in my hand. I came *this* close to dropping it in the waste disposal."

"Please don't do that," he begged. "I promise I

won't be disrespectful again."

"Thank you, Seth. I would appreciate that."

He could almost hear her smiling, her voice suddenly more cheery than before.

"I want the world to know the truth about what happened to Kerry Jones. I want the full video that you shot that night to be released so that everyone can see the faces of those rapists."

"H... h... how do you know who shot the video? It wasn't me."

"I know a lot of things, Seth."

He hesitated for a second, then said what he was thinking but had been too afraid to ask. "Do we know each other?"

The modulated voice sighed.

"The video, Seth. You have until 2 p.m."

"Wait, wait! I've seen the video, but I don't have it," he scrunched his face up in desperation. "It wasn't my camera."

"Then perhaps you know someone who has a copy?"

The call ended.

"Fuck. Fuck! FUCK!" he called over and over again till he reached a crescendo. Letting out his anger didn't make an iota's difference to how fucked he felt.

He landed his wounded fist on the edge of the handbasin. An explosive throb of pain surged through his hand. He winced and clutched his hand to his chest.

"Okay," the manager yelled outside the bedroom

door. "You've had enough warning. I'm coming in."

Seth heard the sound of keys jingling and the lock mechanism turn on the bedroom door.

"I'm coming," Seth screamed. He had no more patience for the idiot at the door.

Seth turned the lock on the bathroom door and stepped into the bedroom. His head whipped from side to side as he took in the horrific scene around him. The bed was covered in a blood splattered plastic sheet that had the negative bloodless imprint of a body lying in the center with legs hanging over the end of the bed. The walls and ceiling were freshly sprayed with spurts of arterial blood. A chair and trash can were pulled up in front of the bed, the trash can lined with a plastic bag full of red soaked tissues.

I am so royally fucked!

Seth looked down at his feet and saw bloody smears where his body had been dragged across the carpet to the bathroom.

The door opened suddenly, and came to a jarring halt about an inch open, stopped by the door chain.

"Open the door," screamed the manager. "I'm not going to ask you again!" He curled his fingers around the door and tried to loosen the chain to no avail.

Seth's heart raced at a million beats a minute. He could hear the blood pulsating through the arteries in his head. He looked around for any evidence, any trace that had been left behind that might help him identify who did this to him. He landed on his knees with a thump and tipped the trash can upside down, searching desperately through its contents. He emptied several scalpel blades, a pair of scissors, suturing needles, and suture holders onto the ground, along with a heap of wet, bloody gauze and dressings.

The manager threw his weight against the door and the chain's screws splintered the wood

"If I have to break the door down you're going to be sorry," said the manager. He thumped the door again with his fist.

Seth got up to his feet and ran back to the bathroom. He locked the door behind him just as the manager broke the chain on the front door and came hurtling into the bedroom.

"What the fuck! What did you do to my room?! You sick fucking bastard!" the manager shouted in disbelief. "You're a fucking dead man!"

Seth slipped the phone into his back pocket, grabbed the last sanitary pad and shoved it in his hoodie pouch,

"Help!" Seth heard the manager shouting outside as he ran from the room. "Somebody help me. Someone's been murdered. Call 911!"

Seth put one foot through the window and found the emergency stairwell with his foot. It felt as if his groin was being ripped apart when he pulled the other foot through the window and made it onto the stairwell landing. His feet missed steps as he tried to reach solid ground as quickly as possible. He landed his left ankle awkwardly as his feet hit the dirt below. Something clicked in the joint and an intense shooting pain travelled up the side of his leg. Every step ached, but at least he could bear weight on his ankle. He prayed it wasn't broken.

The manager was back inside the room again, accompanied by several other men, all shouting at once at the horrific bloody scene. They would have been forgiven for thinking that someone had been murdered in the room. There was so much blood. Seth's blood. The thought made him woozy.

Seth kept close to the building so no one would see him running from the scene of the crime. He crept around the side of the motel and saw a small crowd gathered outside the office reception.

"Are the police coming?" a man yelled over the balcony from the doorway to the room where Seth had come last night with fantasies of getting his rocks off with the hottest chick he'd ever chatted to on a dating app.

"On their way," a lady in the crowd called back.

The manager was swearing repeatedly. He stormed out the room, shaking his head in disbelief.

Seth tried to stay calm, which was easier said than done when he had so much adrenaline and pain killers flooding his system that he could hardly think straight. He tried not to stare at the crowd, but instinct took control of his primitive reflexes and he glanced over his shoulder back toward the motel. An old woman in the crowd caught his stare. She narrowed her eyes and watched him with suspicion.

Fuck! Don't run. Don't do anything stupid.

Parked on the street opposite the motel was a blue 2005 Ford Mustang. His pride and joy. Seth dodged traffic and strode casually toward his car. He closed his eyes and prayed, not to God, but to the universe, that he'd left his keys inside the car because otherwise he was shit out of luck. He was always losing his god damn keys.

He pulled on the handle and the door swung open. Such blessed relief flowed through Seth that he almost cried again. It was about time that luck was on his side.

Or was it all part of the plan?

He cautiously bent over and sat down in the driver's seat without causing himself too much pain. He reached up and tilted the rearview mirror. His reflection scared him. He was pale, sickly, his eyes bloodshot with saggy bags beneath hollow orbs. He shut his eyes for a second and focused, tried to clear his thoughts.

Where did I put my keys?

He'd been so excited when he arrived for the hookup that his memory of shutting the car door and going up to the room was completely hazy.

The glove box only housed a dirty handkerchief that he used to wipe the condensation off the wind-screen on cold Winter mornings, and a half-empty box of condoms. He reached down the side of the doors and came up empty. There was one last place he thought of looking — behind the visor. His whole body shuddered when he found nothing.

He sat in his seat completely defeated. Every part of the cruel torture was so carefully orchestrated. His tormentor had intended for him to feel hope, and to have it slashed away from beneath his feet. Punishment. That's what it was. But to fit what crime? Why the fuck did this psycho want to go and drag up buried dirt like Kerry Jones for? The people involved had been punished enough just knowing that an innocent girl had died. What good would it do anyone for the truth to come out? It wasn't going to bring Kerry back or take away the pain her parents had to go through when their precious eldest daughter removed herself from the human race?

I should go to the cops. Whoever did this has probably already minced what they've taken and rinsed the evidence down the drain.

It sounded like a good idea in his head for only a fraction of a second before a tiny seed of hope and denial sprouted and flourished.

But maybe they haven't. Maybe I'll get my stolen parts back. I just have to follow the instructions. It'll be okay. I wasn't involved. I couldn't give a fuck about those dickheads on the video.

He smacked the steering wheel and stamped his feet in frustration. His foot pressed down on a strange lump beneath the mudguard carpet at his feet. A smile crept across his parched lips. He bent over and pulled aside the carpet.

There they were.

Then he remembered. He didn't want to risk the

chick running off with his keys and stealing his car, so he'd hidden them. But now, in his moment of panic, he'd completely forgotten where that was. It was all starting to come back to him. Seth had never been so happy to find his keys. He snatched them up and clutched them to his chest.

Without his mobile phone he had no way of contacting Mikey. He'd have to visit him in person. The video was something they'd never talked about, but Seth knew Mikey was responsible for releasing it for the whole wide world to see. He never imagined that Mikey would actually edit and release the video, but he did. And if anyone still had a copy, it would be Mikey. He kept almost 3 terabytes of porn on his external hard drives. The guy was a collector who never deleted anything.

The key slid into the ignition and the engine purred to life. One turn of the radio dial and a drum and bass track blared from speakers at the back of the car.

He slipped the bottle of pills down the side of the door, somewhere convenient that he hopefully wouldn't forget them.

He drove away from the motel without looking back. He was terrified that if he did, he might see that lady still watching him, and she would know instantly that it was him, the man from the motel room, the one who was running away.

Where he was in the city, he had no idea. It was a scummy part of town. The kind of streets you imagined you'd get stabbed for a phone and wallet with a twenty inside. Last night, there was something dangerous and sexy about meeting his hookup in a dodgy part of town, but now it just seemed scary.

The phone should have Maps on it, right? Every phone does.

He reached for the phone and opened up the list of apps, found what he was looking for seconds later. The app zoomed in on his location. He'd never visited this part of town before last night. Didn't recognize any of the street names. Didn't want to, either.

Seth heard a scream. He looked up from the phone and saw a lady standing in front of the car, screaming. He slammed on the brakes with only a few feet to go before running her over.

The lady slammed her big fists down on the dashboard. That's when he realized she was no lady. The old tranny in torn leggings, a leather jacket and too much makeup, stormed around the side of the car in her high heels to the driver's side window.

Her voice boomed, "Asshole! You almost killed me!" She spat a large phlegmy glob of spit at his window.

Seth completely freaked out. He put his foot flat on the pedal and drove through the red light. A truck coming through the intersection blared its horn and swerved violently to avoid t-boning Seth's car. The truck smashed through the traffic light on the corner of the road and flipped on its side.

He couldn't stop. He didn't have time.

They'll be okay. The truck wasn't going that fast. The driver will be fine. Whatever cargo the truck was carrying will be covered by insurance. It really wasn't going that fast. The traffic light took most of the impact.

Those were the thoughts that bounced around in Seth's head as he justified the split second decision to drive on, drive faster. He prayed to whatever god that was listening that no one was hurt. They'd helped him today already. Helped him find his keys.

CHAPTER 4

3 Years Earlier

He'd been staring at her all evening. She was sitting in the corner on a sofa by herself, sipping on a glass of water, watching everyone getting rowdy and having fun. Her body language screamed that she felt awkwardly out of place at the party.

"She a freshman?" Seth asked Mikey.

"Which one?"

Seth gestured with a nod in the girl's direction.

Mikey turned his nose up in disapproval.

"Who? Her? Mormon girl?"

"Is she Mormon?"

"No, fuckwit," said Mikey. He stared at her, sizing her up from across the room. "But her pussy comes with at least a one carat entrance fee."

"She turned you down?"

"Nah," said Mikey. "Not interested."

Seth laughed. "Well, have you met me? I'm cute and irresistible."

"Yes, I know all about you, my friend, and your lifetime gift of genital warts."

Seth punched Mikey's arm. "They were penile papules, you dick. The doctor said they were completely normal."

Mikey rubbed his arm vigorously and moaned. "Ah shit, bro, you gave me a dead arm." He swung his arm, letting it flop against his side.

"You deserved it." Seth paused and glanced over at the girl again. "I think I'm gonna go talk to her."

"Knock yourself out. You won't get far with that one."

Seth strolled over and sat down beside the pretty girl he'd had his eye on all night, casually draping his arm across the back of the sofa, behind the girl's head.

"Hey," said Seth.

She brushed her bangs out of her eyes and smiled.

"Hey."

"I'm Seth."

"Kerry."

"Yeah, I know." Seth lied.

She seemed pleasantly surprised.

He aims.

"I couldn't help myself from staring. You look beautiful tonight."

"Thank you," she blushed. "I like your shirt. It's a classic."

Seth pinched the sides of his shirt and looked down at the plain white tee he was wearing.

"Looks better off than on," he said with a wink.

He shoots.

Her smile vanished and she stiffened up.

He doesn't score.

"A little too forward, Romeo."

"You know what I mean." He gave her a lopsided grin.

A second later she giggled and relaxed back in her seat.

Works every time.

"I see you're on the hard stuff," he said, pointing at her glass of water.

"I had way too much to drink tonight. Trying to sober up."

"What's the fun in that?"

She shrugged.

"I saw you here with friends earlier," said Seth.

"They had to get home. I was having fun and wanted to stay."

The girl had a strange definition of fun.

"Sitting on the sofa by yourself? I can think of a few better ways to have fun."

"Like how?"

"Come here, I'll show you."

She leaned toward him. He nudged his jaw out and opened his lips. She closed her eyes and they kissed. She was terrible at first, tight lips and no tongue. But slowly she eased into it. Her plump lips softened, and their silky tongues danced.

Kerry broke the kiss. Her lips were red from rubbing against his stubble.

"I better go," said Kerry.

He gently wrapped his fingers around her wrist and held her hand to his heart. With puppy dog eyes he pleaded. "No. Stay. Please don't leave me. I'll have to go back to hanging out with my dumb friends."

She sighed. "I have an assignment due Tuesday."

She was lying. Seth could tell she was hot for him.

"It's only Friday. I thought you wanted to stay and have fun?"

She smirked and he knew he'd convinced her.

"Let me get you a drink," said Seth. "What do you like?"

"I really should go." She was being coy. It was obvious she wasn't going anywhere.

"Stay here. I insist. What are you drinking?"

"Are there any of those vodka RTDs left?"

"Coming right up."

Seth sprung to his feet and raced for the kitchen, running into Mikey who had been filming the whole thing from the sidelines.

"Well?" asked Mikey. "You getting some tonight?"

"Can you turn the camera off?" said Seth. "And can you delete the bits you recorded of me and Kerry on the sofa."

"Yeah, sure, bro."

Mikey aimed the camera at his feet and flipped the viewfinder shut.

"So you got Mormon girl's name? Nice."

They walked into a quiet corner of the tiny, dated kitchen. Paint was peeling off the warped melamine surfaces. The fridge was so old it probably ran on ammonia. Empty bottles of beer, red solo cups, and food wrappers covered every inch of every surface. Music was pumping from the living room next door, and people were shouting their conversations at one another at the top of their voices to be heard above the noise.

Seth grooved to the music and popped the caps off a couple of bottles of RTD vodka and cherry cola. He took a sniff and recoiled in disgust.

"Smells like cough syrup," said Seth.

"Yeah, but chicks dig that sweet shit," said Mikey.

Seth grinned at him like a naughty schoolboy. He reached inside his pocked and pulled out a small clear bag containing a couple of soy sauce fish bottles.

"Nice," said Mikey.

Seth winked at the camera and took out one of the fish bottles. He opened the small screw lid and squirted the brown contents into one of the RTDs.

Mikey giggled. "You're so messed up, bro."

Seth gave Mikey a wink and reached into the clear bag for another fish bottle.

"No, dude, don't do it," said Mikey, although he said it in a way that sounded like he was egging Seth on.

A couple of squirts and the liquid from the second plastic fish disappeared into the same RTD bottle.

"Someone gonna get some tonight, yo!" Mikey hi-fived Seth.

"You want a couple?" said Seth.

"Nah, bro, I'm good." He tapped the side of his camera and smiled.

Seth pointed a finger at Mikey and put on a stern face. "Make sure you don't film me, okay? I don't want to be part of your little documentary."

"Yeah, man, sure. Of course."

Seth lifted the other RTD and took another sniff. "This stuff is like rocket fuel." He put the bottle to his lips and took a long gulp. "Yuck!" He shook his head and grimaced. "Okay, wish me luck."

The boys fist bumped and Seth made his way back into the heaving living room. Kerry was waiting for him patiently on the sofa. She'd swept her hair back over her shoulder, leaving her neck exposed on one side. He noticed for the first time that she was wearing a silver chain with a crucifix nestled between the upper part of her pert breasts.

It's always the good girls who go for the bad boys. So predictable.

Seth handed her the drink and she took a sip.

"Easy to drink," she said, wiping her moist lips on the back of her hand.

"Cheers," said Seth, and they clinked glasses.

He put his arm on the back of the sofa and then rested it on her shoulders. She took another bigger sip from the RTD and relaxed back against his chest.

"I really like you," said Seth. He brushed the stray hairs behind her ear that were hiding her face.

She smiled. "You, too."

"I was a little scared when you came to talk to me," said Kerry.

"Why is that?"

"You've got a reputation."

Seth laughed. "Oh do I?" Although in his heart he knew it was worse than a reputation. Reputations could be works of fiction. Everything she knew about him was probably true. "Like what?"

"I don't know. That you get with a lot of girls."

"All it means is I haven't found *the one*."

Kerry glanced at him out the corner of her eye. She took another bigger gulp from her drink and her body melted further into the crook of his arm. That line worked *every* time.

"You're beautiful," he said, tilting her chin toward him.

Her eyes were already closed and her lips pouting. They kissed.

Seth grabbed the drink from her hand moments before it tipped and spilled all over the floor. It was empty.

Damn! Girl's a bit of a guzzler.

Seth fetched another couple of drinks for them from the kitchen, and they chatted for hours about everything and nothing in particular. He was really falling for this girl. There was something special about her. The party slowly died down around them as one by one the guests departed, but the two of them were happy in a little world of their own. Seth had completely forgotten about Mikey, and hadn't seen him since they were back in the kitchen.

The longer they talked and kissed, the more dominant Kerry became. Soon, she was the one driving things, sitting on his lap, massaging his pecs, kissing with tongue, and teasing his crotch with her thighs. It was driving Seth wild. He wanted to touch her, but every time he raised his hands to her sides, she placed them behind his head.

She leaned forward and slurred in his ear. "I'm th-still a virgin."

Kerry sat up with her hands on his abs, posed like a cat. She was swaying, drunk... drugged. But Seth had completely forgotten about the *little something extra* he'd slipped into her drink. In that very moment, he had the girl of his dreams rocking on his hips, suggesting... no not suggesting... inviting him to take her virginity.

That's what she meant by that, right?

He didn't care if it was a lie. Girls had used that line on him many times in the past to lure him into their beds. Predators! But he kinda liked being used like that.

He held her close, kissed her neck and worked his way up to her earlobe, which he chewed gently between his lips. "I can show you how," he whispered. "I'll be gentle. Would you like that?"

Kerry nodded and grinned. She was struggling to keep both eyelids open at the same time.

Love drunk, right?

They stood up and Kerry tripped and fell into Seth's arms.

"I'm a little bit drunk," said Kerry. "I don't usually drink this much."

"That's okay," said Seth. She put her arms around his shoulders and he led her through the living room to the hallway, and up the stairs past other couples kissing, to the bedrooms.

Most of the guests at the party were heading in the opposite direction, leaving in cars to go to town to finish off the night in a club. There were only a few stragglers left behind, some even sleeping on the floor, and the desperate few who were picking up abandoned cups in the hunt for more alcohol.

Seth tried the first bedroom door and walked in on a couple of guys fucking doggy style on the bed.

"Get the fuck out man!" yelled one of the guys.

"Sorry, boys," said Seth.

Kerry and Seth giggled like school kids as they closed the door.

"I think I used to go to Sunday school with one of them," said Kerry.

Seth hushed her lips.

"No more talk of Sunday school."

They tried the next bedroom door, which opened

onto a quiet room with only a bedside light on. The walls were covered in baseball posters. The bed wasn't made, but it looked clean enough. They were too drunk to really care anyway.

They flopped down on the bed and made out, their hands exploring each other's body, their lips kissing every square inch of flesh on display. Slowly, they undressed one another down to their underwear.

"You sure you want to do this?" asked Seth.

"Mmm hmm," she bit her bottom lip and swayed seductively in front of him.

Seth reached for his jeans that were lying on the floor. He put his hand into the first pocket and came up empty. He checked the other side pocket, and then the back pockets.

"Fuck, I didn't bring a condom."

Seth pulled open the bedside drawers, found a bottle of lube and a Fleshlight, but no condoms.

"Shit," said Seth. He held his index finger in the air. "Give me one second. I'll be right back."

He literally almost jumped into his jeans, then turned to look at Kerry lying on the bed in her underwear.

She flipped over onto her front. Seth couldn't resist the sight of her bouncy ass, which was impressive for a white girl. Like the apple in the garden of Eden, he had to taste her forbidden fruit. He yanked her panties down to her knees and buried his face between her lips. Just a quick taste before he came back with the condom.

She moaned with pleasure and pushed back against his tongue.

Sweet and delicious. He licked his lips and savored the taste of her.

"I'll be back in a second. Promise."

"Don't go," she moaned.

He quickly put his shirt back on and raced out the room, shutting the door behind him.

He ran to the next bedroom, turned the handle, but the door was locked.

Shit!

The next door was also locked. He dashed to the end of the hallway and opened the door to the bathroom. There was a couple making out in the tub, but they ignored him completely. Seth rummaged through the vanity drawers. At the back of the bottom drawer he found what he was looking for, a box labeled *Magnum-sized*, too. But he was quickly deflated when he opened the box and found only one condom left — and it was opened.

"Sorry, guys," he said to the couple locking faces in the tub.

He made a mad dash down the stairs, skipping over the last remaining couple kissing on the stairs. Downstairs was almost empty. It looked like someone had set a trash explosion off inside the house. Seth was relieved he didn't live in a frat like this. His fraternity would never be stupid enough to open a party to the public like these guys did.

But he was getting distracted. His fingers were

tingling, and every step he took was with a wide gait. He was wrecked from all the alcohol he'd consumed tonight.

I hope I can still get it up. Wouldn't want to disappoint the pretty lady.

Seth rushed through the house trying to find Mikey. There were a lot of guys wearing the college football team letterman jackets. Must have been a football fraternity.

That's right. It's a football frat house. Douchebags.

Mikey was nowhere to be found. Seth checked the downstairs bathroom where a skinny nerd was puking his guts out in the toilet bowl.

"Hey kid, you got a condom?" asked Seth.

The pale, freckled geek gazed up at him with bloodshot eyes and vomit drooling from the side of his mouth. "Do I look like I get laid at parties?"

Seth screwed his face up in disgust and walked back into the living room.

"Come on, Mikey. Where are you, bro?"

He checked the last place he thought Mikey could have been, outside the back of the house smoking a joint. There were a few guys out under a tree having a smoke.

"Any of you guys seen Mikey?"

"Who the fuck is Mikey?" said one of the douchebags in a letterman.

"Never mind," said Seth, turning around and heading back inside the house.

Seth sulked as he walked back up the stairs.

Looks like I'm only getting head tonight.

There was a small commotion going on at the top of the stairs, guys in letterman jackets clambering to see inside one of the bedroom doors.

"Oh shit," said one of the guys, beaming with excitement, "He's really giving it to her."

The guys were all crowded outside the room where he'd left Kerry lying on the bed.

"What's going on?" asked Seth.

"This slutty girl was lying ass up in bed for the taking. My bro already dumped a load," said one of the football jocks, nudging his tall teammate in the ribs. "If you want a turn, you gotta wait at the back of the line."

Seth stood on his tiptoes and stared into the room. A guy was taking Kerry from behind, his hairy ass clenching hard with every thrust. There was another guy sitting in front of Kerry, leaning back against the headboard, his legs spread, one arm folded behind his head while he held a handful of Kerry's hair in the other hand, bobbing her mouth on his crotch.

"Smile for the boys," said Mikey.

Seth stood as tall as he could and saw Mikey inside the room, filming the whole thing.

"What the fuck, Mikey?" Seth said softly to himself.

"Yeah sweet cheeks, smile for the camera," said the guy getting a blowjob. He turned her head and made her look at the camera. Her eyes were barely open, nothing registering.

I thought she liked me. Why would she let them do that to her?

"Fucking slut," Seth grumbled and turned to leave.

"The way we like them!" said one of the football boys, raising his beer and cheering. The other guys all cheered and clinked beers. One of them already had his dick out, hard in his hand, edging slowly into the room for his turn.

Seth walked down the stairs, defeated. Lost in a whirlwind of self pity and raging hormones that now had no release, he didn't see a girl standing in his way and walked straight into her.

"I'm so sorry," said Seth.

"That's okay," she replied. "I didn't see you either."

He wandered downstairs, passing the group of guys who had been outside smoking weed, who were now heading upstairs to check out the action. The aftermath of the party was horrendous. The place was completely trashed, drink stains on the sofas, half drunk cups of beer everywhere, food pressed into the carpet.

It was eerily quiet downstairs, making him suddenly aware of the ringing in his ears. But at least it drowned out the sounds coming from upstairs. The disgusting sex sounds of the girl he'd wanted so badly giving herself over to those other guys like a cheap whore.

Those douchebags. That slut!

He sat on one of the three seater sofas and stared

blankly at the television silently playing music videos in front of him, devastated. The girl he passed on the stairs sat down on the seat beside him, bouncing on the cushion.

"Are you having a good night?"

Seth gave her a look that should have been clear he wasn't interested in talking to her, but she persisted.

"I've had such a good time. This is the first frat party I've been to. Have you been to one of these before? Of course you have, you're a sophomore right? I'm a freshman. Just started Psychology this year. Moved here from New York. Wanted to get away from the big city. What are you studying?"

Did the girl ever stop to breathe? He interrupted her mid-sentence with a kiss. Seth didn't know why he did it. He didn't fancy her in the slightest. She was a little too frumpy and ordinary for his taste. One of those annoying people who had to fill the silence with her incessant talking when she got nervous. He was willing to bet real money that she had smelly feet.

But when he closed his eyes he saw Kerry. He tasted Kerry on the fat girl's lips. He ran his hands over her big round boobs and she *was* Kerry.

"Oh, that's nice," she said.

He put a finger to her lips and shushed her before the moment was forever ruined by her irritating voice.

Seth lay his body on top of the girl and kissed her deeply with tongue. She moaned and the small vibrations from her vocal cords travelled to his skin and tickled his lips. What she lacked in looks, she definitely made up in kissing ability. A girl like her wouldn't exactly have had the boys chasing her down the streets, so he assumed she was a natural. He wondered what else she was a natural at?

Seth closed his eyes and he was once again in Kerry's arms. He could picture that beautiful wide smile of hers so perfectly in his head. He wanted her so badly, it was obvious from the bulge in his pants. The girl wrapped her legs around his waist and suddenly he was completely transported into his fantasy.

Kerry looked back at him.

"I want you to fuck me, Seth. Fuck me hard. I'm ready for you."

He was only too happy to oblige. He fumbled with his belt while still kissing her sweet lips. Kerry helped him unfix the clasp and his pants were swiftly down to his knees.

She squealed into her palm as he entered her a little too roughly.

"Oh my god," she cried out.

He put the palm of his hand over her mouth to stop her from speaking again. The moment had almost been ruined.

Seth realized that he'd entered her too soon. She wasn't wet yet, and the dry walls of her womanhood tugged uncomfortably as he forced himself inside her, over and over again. But it was what Kerry wanted.

She'd asked him to do it, and he was more than happy to oblige.

Kerry lay there staring up at him with a smile on her face and a look of endless love in her eyes. His breathing quickened and every muscle in his groin contracted at once as he came prematurely inside her. Kerry tipped her head back and moaned into his hand.

He was angry at himself. For letting himself get carried away when he was just starting to enjoy it. He hated when it happened, and this wasn't the first time either. It was all over so quickly.

Seth looked down at the startled girl lying beneath him on the sofa. He took his hand off her mouth, leaving a white imprint from his tight grip. They said nothing to one another as she slipped out from under him and pulled on her panties.

He put on his pants and tucked in his shirt.

They stared in opposite directions for a few seconds.

"Thanks," Seth said abruptly as he stood up and left the room.

He could hear every thrust and groan coming from upstairs as he headed for the front door. Did Kerry have no self respect at all?

Seth stood on the spot, frozen. He contemplated whether to do something heroic? If he raced in there and tried to protect her dignity, maybe even punched someone, he would likely end up in the Emergency

Department. He was outnumbered by the football jocks at least 10 to 1.

No. She was on her own. She chose to be a slut. She could have had Seth but she chose the football jocks. She couldn't blame it all on the drugs. They only brought out the real you, the true you, lowering your inhibitions. It was all an act, that sweet doe-eyed country girl she pretended to be. She was damaged goods now. Probably lied about being a virgin to get in his pants. He could never date a girl like that. He'd never be able introduce her to his parents as his sweet Kerry. That dream was well and truly dead.

She got what she deserved. She could have had me.

Seth turned on his heels and walked out the frat house, closing the door behind him, and shutting out the disgusting sounds of flesh slapping together in the heat of copulation.

CHAPTER 5

Present Day

Seth gently put his foot on the brake as he turned down Mikey's street. Grandiose houses towered over high fences and bushy shrubs that lined their borders. Every house had an SUV parked in the driveway, swimming pool out back, and perfectly manicured lawns. It was a suburban cliché.

Seth's parents had run into financial difficulty a year ago. They told everyone they'd sold their house to take advantage of soaring prices, but really they couldn't afford the mortgage. His dad had lost the family's savings on amateur stock market trading — his mom called it gambling — leaving them living month to month off wages alone. Seth had to move out of his studio apartment near campus, and back home. From having a revolving door of endless hot chicks, to being treated like a kid and made to do chores. It was the ultimate punishment for a young guy who'd been given a taste of freedom.

The family had moved into a nice apartment uptown, where Seth had a massive bedroom overlooking the city with an en-suite all to himself, at least that's the story Seth told everyone about how they now lived in a penthouse apartment. Promises were made that he'd host a big party there one weekend when the parentals were away, but the truth was his dad's best friend had taken pity on them and rented his 3 bedroom, first floor apartment in Chinatown to the family for a fraction of the market price.

Seth parked up opposite Mikey's house. His crotch felt wet but luckily nothing had leaked through the sanitary pad onto his jeans. He opened the door and climbed out, his head spinning from the change in posture. Seth lay his head in his hands on the roof of the car and shut his eyes.

"You okay, mister?" said a lady passing by walking her two miniature poodles.

Seth jumped at the sound of her voice. He spun around and closed the car door.

She was a mid-forties suburban housewife, wearing tight baby blue Lululemon active wear and pink Nike shoes that matched her pink Nike peak cap. Her bleached blonde hair was pulled up in a ponytail, and her makeup was perfect. She was a babe.

"Yeah," he said. "All peachy, thanks."

She looked him up and down. It was obvious that she wanted to say something else, but she kept it to herself, and increased her pace. The little dogs growled and yapped at Seth as the lady dragged them along behind her.

Seth pushed the button on the intercom at the gate and waited for a reply. He stared up at the camera mounted high on one of the gateposts. His friendship with Mikey had been tenuous ever since the Valentine's Day events. They called each other "best friends", but the bromance they had shared before the events of that night was never the same again.

"Come on in, buddy," Mikey said over the intercom.

The gates swung open, and Seth walked up the driveway to the front door.

Mikey was already standing in the open doorway when Seth reached the house.

"What brings you to this neck of the woods? You miss the burbs? You haven't visited in weeks." Mikey smirked and then waved Seth into the house. "You look like shit, man."

"I'm fine." But Seth didn't look or sound fine at all.

Mikey gave him a quizzical glance over his shoulder and led Seth to the living room where he'd been camped out playing video games all day. Mikey threw himself onto one of the bean bags he had positioned in front of the TV.

"Take a seat," said Mikey, pointing at the bean bag beside his own.

Seth couldn't, even if he wanted to. He was afraid if he lay down he wouldn't be able to get up again without ripping through every stitch in his groin. A cold shiver ran through him, and his body broke out in a fine sweat.

"You okay, buddy?" said Mikey. "You look like you're sick. Or are you wasted?"

"No," said Seth. "Like I said, I'm fine."

Mikey turned his attention to the game that he'd had paused. He carried on with his Call of Duty mission, fingers bashing the controller, eyes glued to the screen.

"No, no, no," Mikey yelled as two characters blind-sided him and took him out. He turned his head and snapped at Seth. "I can't concentrate on my game with you standing there like that. It's distracting."

Seth came out and said it. "I need a copy of the video you made of Kerry Jones."

Mikey's fingers slipped off the controls and his character perished in a shower of bullets. This time, Mikey didn't say anything. After a moment he looked at Seth.

"Why?"

"You still got it, right?"

"Why do you want it?"

Seth didn't know what to say. Did he tell his ex-best friend that he'd been castrated and the only way to get his bits back was to show the world what really happened that night to sweet Kerry Jones? Why the fuck would Mikey care whether or not Seth ever got to shower naked in public again? Mikey was on that tape, and Seth should have known he wouldn't just hand it over.

"I want to watch it. The whole thing. I never got to see it. Only the watered down version you put on the internet."

Mikey narrowed his gaze ever so slightly, studying Seth's face.

"Why now?"

Stay calm. Don't look desperate.

Mikey hit a button on his controller and launched his character back into the heat of action.

"Nah, bro, deleted it months ago. Didn't want it hanging around after all the shit that went down afterward."

"You mean when she killed herself?"

Mikey's jaw clenched.

"I think we should give it to the cops," said Seth. He wanted to stop himself from saying it, but the words flowed like vomit.

Mikey threw his controller onto the ground and sprung up to his feet. He grabbed Seth by the scruff of his neck and shoved him backward a few steps.

"Are you fucking kidding me?" Mikey yelled. "What the fuck is wrong with you, man? You're on something, I can tell. You look fucked out of your mind. Your pupils are the size of pin heads."

"So you've got it then?"

Seth knew he wasn't helping matters by

confronting Mikey, but it was his impulsive nature to jump first and ask questions later.

"I deleted it, okay?" said Mikey.

"Mother fucker." Seth gave Mikey a rough shove.

Mikey threw a punch but Seth saw it coming. He leaned away from the flying fist, Mikey's knuckles grazing the five o'clock shadow on his jawline. Seth threw himself on top of Mikey. The two of them crashed down onto the ground. Mikey's knee connected with his wound and Seth instantly regretted what he'd done. He may have had the upper hand, but the pain was too blindingly intense for him to carry on fighting. He rolled up into a ball in the fetal position and cried.

Mikey jumped up to his feet, ready to throw another punch, but he'd already won.

"What the fuck is wrong with you, man? Get the fuck out of my house!" Mikey pointed at the door and bellowed.

Seth pushed himself up onto all fours, choking on sobs, drool running from the corners of his mouth.

"Please help me," Seth begged.

Mikey raised his arm as if to backhand Seth across the face, but froze with his hand mid-air.

"Get out!" said Mikey bluntly.

"Please, Mikey."

But it was too late the moment he'd suggested they hand the video over to the cops. Nothing he could say would have been able to persuade Mikey to show him the video after that.

"Don't make me say it again," said Mikey, gesturing with his hand in the direction of the front door.

Seth blubbered as he pushed himself up onto his knees and finally onto two feet. A broken man, he stumbled back the way he came. By the time he reached the front door, he could hear Mikey blasting enemies on his Playstation and swearing at the TV screen.

Sitting beside the front door was a bowl of keys, and attached to each keyring was a remote control for opening the electric front gates. He reached into the bowl and took the first set of keys that his fingers could find and slipped them straight into his pocket.

Seth pushed the intercom buzzer beside the front door and the entrance gates started to swing open. He pulled the front door shut behind him with more force than necessary, but he wanted to make a point of slamming it hard so Mikey would know that he'd left the premises.

The walk to the car felt like a marathon. Sweat was starting to pool on his brow and with every step he grew more lightheaded and nauseated. His hands shook as he tried to line the key up with the ignition. Eventually, he managed to start the engine and drive a short distance down the street where he had a clear view of Mikey's driveway, but was far enough away not to be noticed. Mikey's street had a cul-de-sac at the end, so he was certain Mikey wouldn't end up driving by and find him laying in wait.

Seth switched off the engine and let his head lay back against the headrest. His lids became heavy and the sweet escape of sleep beckoned him into its comforting embrace. Minutes later, he collapsed in the front seat of his car and passed out.

CHAPTER 6

The sound of a car alarm bleeping woke Seth up with a start. He jumped in his seat and looked around. Confused at first, it took a moment for him to get his bearings and recognize where he was. He slunk down behind the steering wheel and tried to stay out of sight. He'd been woken by one of the neighbors coming home and setting her car alarm off by mistake.

What time is it?

He looked at his watch.

14:38

"You fucking idiot!" he swore at himself and slammed the steering wheel with his palms. In the rearview mirror he saw a sickly pale version of himself staring back at him.

The pills.

"The fucking pills!"

They weren't in his trouser pockets, or his jacket pockets.

"Come on," he said in desperation. "Be here, please be here." He turned up the piles of books and clothes sitting on the back seats.

Then he remembered where he'd put them, down the side of the door. He screwed off the top of the bottle and tipped out a handful.

He was due to take one of the pills, he was certain of that much. At first the pain had been the biggest concern, but now the nausea and shakes were taking hold and he was starting not to care very much about the throbbing ache down below.

"Did she say to take the white one every four hours or the blue one? Or was it every six hours?" He clutched his face in despair. "I don't remember."

Seth panicked and made a split second decision. He gulped down one of each color pill. Part of him hoped he'd instantly feel better, but nothing changed. Seth tipped one of each color pill into his hand and then placed them in his pocket. The rest went back down the side of the door.

A tiny bird started tweeting — *Tweet tweet, tweet tweet.*

Where is that fucking annoying sound coming from?

The notification light was flashing on the smartphone from the motel that he'd left on the dash.

"1 new message"

Anger simmered deep within Seth's soul. The things he planned to do to whoever was responsible for this when he finally got his hands on them, and he'd been given his dick back. They'd be begging for him to end the pain. Every bit of it justified for what they'd done to him.

Another cold sweat and shudder.

Seth tapped on the message. There was an image attached to the text of a glass jar containing a large pale white pickle in a plastic bag buried in ice.

Oh, jesus, that's not a pickle.

— Time is running out

As if he needed any further reminding.

A sound caught his attention. A car engine purred to life a few houses down, and drum and bass polluted the quiet suburban air. It was Seth's favorite song from an obscure band that he and Mikey used to listen to all the time. Mikey was on his way out.

Seth watched from a distance, staring intently at Mikey's front gate, hoping he wasn't just imagining things.

He was in luck. The gates swung open and Mikey

drove out in the Ford F-Series his parents had bought him for his twentieth birthday, without slowing down to look for pedestrians or other cars. Mikey revved his engine and switched down a gear. Tires screamed as the truck roared down the road.

This is it. This is my chance.

The afternoon air became still again as the sounds of Mikey's truck drifted off into the distance. There was no one walking down this quiet side street, and most of the residents would have been at work. Seth put the phone in his pocket and climbed out of his car. He casually strode toward Mikey's house. His heart fluttered as he reached out his hand and pushed the remote control.

The gates opened and his whole body shuddered. Something was very wrong with him. He was sick. He'd never felt this unwell, this light headed, and this desperate to crawl into bed and go to sleep for a very long time. He didn't need to be a doctor to know he was septic. But he'd worry about that later.

He plodded up the driveway to the front of Mikey's house. When he reached the front door, he had the sudden realization that unless the set of keys he stole had a key to the house, then he was shit out of luck. He held the keys in the air and stared at them through blurry eyes. There were at least three different keys on the set that might have been a good fit. He leaned his shoulder against the door to support himself from falling over, and tried each key. It took agonizingly long for him to focus enough through the chills and shakes to try the keys, and luck was on his side. The second key slipped cleanly into the slot. One revolution and the internal mechanism let out the *click* that Seth was so desperate to hear.

He turned the handle and stepped into the house. The TV was still playing in the background in the living room. Seth knew that Mikey's parents were almost never at home this early during the day. He stumbled down the hallway to the living room, resting one shoulder on the wall for support. On the floor, beside the Playstation controller was an empty plastic bag with the dregs of Mikey's marijuana stash.

He's gone out to buy more weed.

And Seth knew exactly where Mikey would be going, the same place they always went downtown. It meant Mikey would be gone for at least an hour. Seth had the time he needed to find the video.

He knew Mikey wouldn't have deleted the video. It had to be on one of his infamous hard drives.

The march up the stairs to Mikey's bedroom seemed insurmountable, but Seth took it one step at a time. Whichever pill was the painkiller, it was starting to work, and giving Seth a double ass kicking. If only the antibiotic would start working.

Mikey's room was down the far end of the house. His parents had given him the wing of the house that they'd built for his grandmother to live in while she was alive. It had its own bathroom and living room, but his parents wouldn't let him keep a TV in there. If they did, they knew he'd never venture forth from his man cave, except for meals.

The door to Mikey's room was closed but the handle turned easily. A damp smell of boy musk assaulted Seth's senses like an archaeologist opening up a sealed mass grave. Bile rose in his dry throat, burning the back of his mouth. He'd only ever been up here once before, when Mikey's family moved into the house. Mikey preferred to entertain his guests downstairs. The reason was now obvious.

No fucking wonder!

Animals took better care of where they slept at night than Mikey did. His room wasn't so much a floordrobe as a nest of clothes, food wrappers, and discarded Kleenex. Smoldering below the stench of dirty clothes, was the gag inducing bleachy odor of stale cum. Seth felt gross just breathing in the air. There were probably vaporized particles of Mikey's semen floating all around him, impregnating his lungs with each breath. If he woke up in nine month's time and had a baby Mikey foot shoving its way out of his chest like that thing from *Aliens,* he wouldn't have even been surprised. Mikey was fucking feral.

Unfortunately, he needed to find the hard drives, and he wouldn't have any choice but to touch items in the room. The one clear area of the bedroom was around the computer; a beast of a machine built specifically for gaming, editing movies, and watching shit tons of porn. The surface of the desk was clear except for a keyboard and mouse. There was no sign of Mikey's precious external hard drives. There was shit on there that could get him arrested, or so he used to tell the other guys when he was bragging about his collection. Seth always laughed, but secretly, deep down in inside, was a little concerned. There was only a handful of stuff that could get you arrested, and he really hoped Mikey wasn't into that kind of rank shit.

Another cold chill ran down Seth's spine. He felt woozy and his skin got all clammy.

Outside, a car alarm blared. A surge of adrenaline squirted from his adrenals to his heart, and like an explosion dispersed through his arteries to every inch of his flesh. Clarity came to him, and for a moment the grogginess faded and the pain was nothing more than background noise.

"Shit," he mumbled.

I gotta be quick. If that's him then I'm screwed. But it can't be him. How long has it been since he left?

Seth checked his watch. Mikey had been gone for almost twenty minutes. He should still have had plenty of time.

Unless he didn't.

What if he's forgotten something? Shit! Caught red handed.

Seth ran to the window and peered out. He had a clear line of sight down the driveway and into the next door neighbor's yard. The neighbor was pointing her car alarm remote at her black Nissan X Trail, failing to silence the alarm. She threw her arms up in frustration and marched back into her house.

Relief. There was no other word to describe what Seth felt. Sheer blessed relief.

The hard drive had to be in the room somewhere, and thinking logically for a second, somewhere near the computer. He pulled open the desk drawers, shifted piles of clothes as he rummaged through everything within a few feet of the desk.

It has to be here somewhere.

Seth stopped to think. If he were a porn addicted slob who didn't want anyone to find his contraband, where would he hide his hard drives.

Under my mattress.

His hand slipped under the grimy mattress. He reached all the way up to his elbow, then further until his entire arm was sandwiched between the mattress and the base. Then he struck gold, the outline of something rectangular and plastic at the end of his fingertips. His fingers just managed to grip the edge of the hard drive to pull it out from under the mattress. He held the black box with more joy than he'd experienced in years. Better than the Xbox One his parents had got him for Christmas a few years back.

The phone began to ring, and he dropped the hard drive on the bed.

"555-0135 calling"

Seth's whole body tensed in fear and he lost control of his bladder. Urine burned the gash between his legs as it cascaded out of him, saturating the sanitary pad and soaking his pants. His legs shook like wobbly jelly and caved at the knees. Warm urine ran down the inside of his thighs and pooled on the carpet at his knees.

He wanted to die. For it all to be over and not have to go on fighting this misery.

Seth answered the phone.

"What do you want?" he said coldly through gritted teeth.

The modulated voice took a deep breath in and out.

"Hello to you, too, Seth. What I want is for you to succeed at your task. I want you to redeem yourself."

Nostrils flared and his chest heaved with fury.

"Now I don't want to be the bearer of bad news, but you're running out of time. There are still two tasks ahead of you, and not very many more hours before it's too late. Hurry, Seth."

The phone went dead.

"Fuck!" he cursed and threw the phone onto the carpet. Instantly regretting his actions, he scooped it up in his hands and checked that it was still working. It was.

Thank god.

He ripped off his saturated, foul smelling jeans and tossed them amongst the mess of clothes on Mikey's floor. The smell would blend right in with the other disgusting fumes marinating in the room. The sanitary pad was stuck to his groin like glue. He peeled it away, gagging at the sight of blood and yellowish *pussy* discharge.

"No wonder I feel sick."

He reached into his pocket for the spare pills he'd brought with him, popped another white and blue one in his mouth. His throat was bone dry, and the pills scratched his esophagus like sandpaper on soft skin. His throat clenched into a tight spasm and he choked. Seth dashed for the en-suite, his hands flailing about in front of him to turn on the water. The glass beside the hand basin tumbled and smashed on the floor, shards flying across the grubby white tiles. He scooped up a handful of water and swallowed the pills down, then slowly tiptoed his way out of the bathroom, avoiding any shiny reflective specks of glass.

In his pocket he had the spare sanitary pad. He walked back into the bedroom and stared at his reflection in the full length mirror attached to the wardrobe. Those times as a young boy when he'd pretended to be a girl by slipping his dick and balls between his legs and squeezing them tightly together — that's exactly what he looked like now. Seth didn't want to take a closer look, but he knew he had to. If there was an infection, he needed to get medical attention. He stepped up to the mirror and opened his legs as wide as the pain allowed. Some of the stitches had pulled apart, but for the most part the wound had held together, scabbed at the edges, and surrounded by a perimeter of reddened skin. It was definitely infected.

Seth took the spare sanitary pad from his pocket and put it between his legs and held it in place. He opened Mikey's cupboard and hoped he'd find at least one pair of clean pants. They had a similar body shape, so he figured he'd be in luck. And he was. Hanging up in front of him were three identical pairs of dark blue jeans. Tentatively, he opened Mikey's wardrobe drawers. The first drawer he closed almost instantly when he saw a big purple dong, glow in the dark sex dice, and a bottle of lube. The second drawer down he was in luck. Three brand spanking new, unopened boxes of white undies. Rather than clean his clothes, Mikey, the spoilt little shit that he was, obviously just bought several of the same item when he found something he liked.

Seth ripped open one of the boxes and stole a pair of boxer briefs. He put them on and they held the pad securely against his gash. The jeans were an almost perfect fit, hanging ever so loosely on his hips, but at least they were clean and dry.

There was no more time to waste. Seth grabbed a clean set of socks from Mikey's drawers, and found a new t-shirt that still had the smell of formaldehyde all over it. He quickly changed his clothes, tossing the old, filthy ones aside. Mikey had a bottle of cologne on his bedside table. It was the closest thing to a shower that Seth had time for, dousing himself in Armani Code.

The computer was in standby mode. Seth plugged the external hard drive into a spare USB slot and moved the mouse. A message sprung up asking for a password to unlock the account. The account name on the screen read "*Porn**". Seth rolled his eyes.

Porn star? How does he even get laid? If this is what his room looks like, imagine what's living under his foreskin.

Seth gagged and tried to suppress the very explicit image in his mind of his ex-best friend's smegmous cock and some poor, unsuspecting babe getting down on her knees, wondering what that festering smell was as she unfolded his foreskin to take his cheesy knob into her mouth.

As far as he could see, there were two options. Try to hack into Mikey's computer with an infinite number of possibilities, or take the hard drive and run.

It's worth a shot just trying, right?

So he sat down at the computer and hit the return key.

Nothing happened.

Wrong password.

He typed Mikey's birthday and hit the return key.

Nothing happened.

Wrong password.

"Fuck it," he said, going for the obvious.

Seth typed "password" and hit the return key.

The desktop screen appeared. It was blank except for a link to Mikey's Cloud storage account and a folder called *Hardcore* that must have been the external hard drive.

Why am I friends with this moron?

He clicked on the *Hardcore* folder and a list of files as long as the phone directory loaded. The titles mostly resembled the inane click-baity titles on "free" porn sites; *Daddy does his little girl up the ass, Girl takes two loads on her tits, Anal ass bandits*, the kind of stuff his generation had grown so used to watching it was mainstream and had zero shock value.

Then he came across a folder with a title that seemed out of place — *Temp.*

Seth opened the folder and his skin crawled. The word *rape* repeated over and over. It gave Seth the creeps.

What sort of sick shit is Mikey into?

He ran a search through the folder for the word "Kerry".

— 2 results

— Kerry Jones Valentine's Day rape (uncut) HOT 4h27m
— Kerry Jones Valentine's Day gangbang (edited) 3m20s

The cursor hovered over the files for a few seconds. His finger wavering with trepidation. Then he clicked on the uncut version. The video started playing. He was on the screen, sitting beside Kerry Jones on the sofa at the party, smiling and chatting. From where Mikey had been standing with the camera he didn't manage to capture any of the audio, but from the smiles, the body language, Kerry hanging on every word that Seth said, it was obvious the two had chemistry.

What was that strange sensation in his chest? A queasy uneasiness that left him so unsettled.

The video jumped to various shots of the frat party from that night. Most of the faces were recognizable. At first, Mikey's camera followed Seth around the party like he was the star of a reality TV show. But soon the footage changed to inane crowd shots, and closeups of pretty girls' chests. Every now and then, Mikey's camera stole glimpses of Kerry through the crowd.

Seth started to realize something that hadn't been clear to him before. Did Mikey also have a crush on Kerry? Sure, ninety percent of what he'd seen so far was of the two boys having a laugh, but Kerry got more screen time than any other girl at the party. And it wasn't her rack or ass that he zoomed in on, it was her face, her lips, her smile. Seth had been so blinded by his own feelings that he never saw how much his best friend wanted the same girl.

He skipped ahead, ten minutes at a time. Slowly,

the crowded house cleared out, the lights dimmed, and it was only the drunks and stragglers left behind. He stopped at the part where Mikey filmed him leading Kerry upstairs. But it wasn't how he remembered it. She wasn't that hot and horny freshman chasing him up to the bedroom for a wild night of uncomplicated fun, followed by whatever the future held for them as a couple. No, she set one foot up the stairs after another like a dazed zombie.

Seth couldn't watch any more. He knew how the movie ended.

Out of nowhere, he felt as if he had the weight of the world on his shoulders pressing down on him, and the guilt of what finally became of Kerry Jones dragged him even deeper. The feeling that was bearing down on him, he knew what it was... responsibility... culpability. He'd never wanted to acknowledge that he'd played a part in her downfall... and death. But he couldn't live in blissful ignorance any longer.

Even though he wasn't one of the guys who raped her and ruined her life, he played an essential role in the events that led to the tragedy, possibly even bearing the sole responsibility for striking the match that set off a chain reaction of events leading to the death of a girl he could have fallen in love with had the circumstances been different.

"You sick fucking bastard," said Seth as he clicked the small x in the corner of the video to close it. "You deserve everything that you have coming to you."

He opened up a browser window and logged into his Cloud account. For the fifteen minutes it took the video to upload, he sat in silence, stupefied by the might of his selfishness. As soon as the upload was complete, he copied the share link.

They won't be able to trace this to me? Will they?

He quickly clicked back to his Cloud account and checked. It was an anonymous link and no one would be able to trace the file to him.

He browsed to the local newspaper website. There was a link on the homepage for members of the public to make anonymous tips. He clicked it, and in the small text box that appeared he pasted the address to the video.

Send

Oh my god, what have I done?

Euphoria and terror hit him at once. The bastards who destroyed a sweet and innocent girl's life were about to have hell rained down upon them, but he knew there would be fallout for himself too. While he'd been smart enough not to let Mikey film him slipping the drugs into the girl's drink, there was footage of him leading her upstairs, even if he was only up there for a couple of minutes.

But it was too late to go back.

Another cold shiver.

I feel like I'm going to be sick. I need to get a different antibiotic. This one isn't working anymore.

CHAPTER 7

The nearest drugstore was a few miles from Mikey's house. Seth pushed through the front door and a bell chimed above his head.

"Just a minute," a cheery voice called out from the small office behind the counter.

A middle-aged woman with red and grey streaked hair who wore oversized glasses stepped out. She smiled and her face wrinkled up in a hundred places.

"You're in luck," said the pharmacist. "I'm running about two hours late for my lunch and was about to head out, but I forgot to lock the door. What can I help you with? Itch a scratch don't fix? Burrrn when you pass the urrrn?" She shielded her mouth with the back of her hand as if she was telling a secret. "Condoms? We stock in every size from itty bitty to donkey dick. Safety first."

"I don't need condoms," said Seth.

The pharmacist, whose name badge read "*Judy*", frowned as she gave Seth a good once over. Her expression changed to one of concern and she leaned over the counter.

"Honey, are you alright? You look like death warmed up."

"I feel terrible."

"You taken any drugs? Your pupils are kinda teeny." She held her thumb and index finger a fraction apart.

"Painkillers," he said, now swaying on his feet.

"I can't sell you any more painkillers. I'm sorry."

"I don't need painkillers. I need antibiotics. Whatever they gave me isn't working."

"Whatever *who* gave you?" Judy's brow furrowed ever deeper with concern.

Seth tried to focus on her face, but he was getting terrible double vision and everything was blurry.

"Honey? Don't faint on me. Don't you dare!"

Judy threw open the door in the counter that separated the two of them, and rushed to support Seth as he slumped to the ground.

"Help!" screamed Judy. "Somebody call 911. Help!" A passerby rushed into the drug store.

"What happened?"

"Quick! There's a phone behind the counter. Call 911."

It was the last thing Seth was aware of before everything turned black.

CHAPTER 8

Lights flashed before his eyes and there was a distant echo of voices talking around him, about him. A man in blue scrubs was standing on one side of him, and a lady in green scrubs and a white lab coat on the other, pushing him on a stretcher, bright lights zooming by above his head.

"Patient is a 20-year-old male, febrile at 101, tachycardic, hypotensive ninety over sixty. Heart sounds dual, chest clear, no obvious focus of infection. GCS now fourteen out of fifteen, was GCS eleven when the paramedics arrived. Was on a naloxone infusion on the way here, but narcosis has resolved. He's got IV fluids running and was given a dose of Rocephin stat in the ambulance. Point of care hemoglobin was less than ninety," said the man in blue scrubs.

"Sounds like he's lost a lot of blood and he's septic." The lady rubbed Seth on the shoulder. "Sir, can you hear me? My name is Sally, I'm one of the doctors. You're in the Emergency Department at Saint Margaret's. Can you tell me your name?"

"I... I need to go," Seth mumbled.

"You're very sick. We think the best place for you right now is in hospital," said Sally.

Staring up into the lights whizzing by made Seth nauseous, so he shut his eyes.

"You need to try to keep your eyes open. Can you hear me? What's your name?" She spoke in a calm voice to the nurse. "Can you get me another 18 gauge IV line please?"

"Seth," he said. "My name's Seth."

"Seth, do you have any pain anywhere?"

"Yes."

"Where Seth?"

He had tears in his eyes but he couldn't tell her the truth.

"Where's the pain, Seth?" After a few seconds Sally gave up trying. "Give him 50 micrograms of fentanyl. I don't want him overdosing on opiates again." She leaned over Seth again. "Any cough? Or phlegm?"

"No."

His head lolled from one side to the other.

"Where is the pain, Seth?"

So much pain. As if all the analgesia he'd taken had been drained from his body. But he didn't want to tell her. If she looked at his groin she'd want to keep him in hospital, and... he didn't even want to think about what might happen if he was stuck there and his time ran out.

"No," he shook his head, grinding his teeth to stop from crying out.

"Right," said Sally, not sounding convinced. She spoke in a soft voice to the man in blue scrubs. "Do we know if he had any drugs on him?"

"Pockets were empty," said the man.

Seth squinted through the bright light at the man's name badge. He was a nurse named "*Kevin*".

"And he collapsed in a drug store? Asking for antibiotics? Strange."

"That's the story that was handed over to me," said Kevin.

Sally sighed. "Run a full septic screen, chest x-ray and blood cultures. He seems confused to me. I'll order a head CT. Let's hit him hard with broad spectrum antibiotics until the cultures come back. Load him up with IV fluids. He may need a catheter."

Alarm bells started ringing in Seth's head.

A catheter? No! They can't put a catheter in!

They parked the hospital bed in a quiet corner of the ED.

"Thanks, Sally," said Kevin.

"No problem. Page me if there are any concerns. I'll chase the results."

Sally left the bedside as Kevin pulled up Seth's shirt to place ECG electrodes. He attached a small device that looked like a clothes peg to Seth's fingertip and a monitor started beeping with the rhythm of his heart. It didn't sound good. His heart was galloping at a hundred miles an hour.

"You're gonna be alright, bro." Kevin gave Seth a rub on the shoulder and a smile. "We'll take good care of you. Just have to ask one question." Kevin dropped down to eye level with Seth at the side of the bed. "Is there anything you want to tell me that you couldn't share with the doctor? Anything maybe... illegal?"

Yes! Yes. Some psycho cut off my dick and balls and now I'm a fucking eunuch! If I don't get out of here soon they're going to throw them down the drain and I don't know if I want to keep living if life is going to be like this.

"No," he replied, sobbing gently.

"It's okay, bro. You're pretty unwell. There weren't any numbers saved on your phone. We tried calling back the last number who called you but when they answered they didn't say anything. Hung up after a few seconds."

Seth sniggered. He was so utterly fucked right now.

"You may have heard the doctor talking about a catheter..."

Kevin reached out to unbutton Seth's jeans. Seth shot up a hand and caught Kevin's wrist in a tight clench.

"Hands off, buddy," Seth said coldly.

Kevin jerked back in surprise, pulling his hand free of Seth's grip. He rubbed his red wrist.

"I'm only trying to help," said Kevin. He stormed

away in a huff, muttering to himself "Feel free to piss your pants if you prefer. Asshole!"

"Sorry," Seth said softly, and he really did mean it. He'd been a dick to that guy, who didn't deserve it. The nurse was only trying to help.

I have to get out of here.

Already he felt infinitely better than before. That ever-present sick sense of dread and exhaustion had dissipated. The pain was still there, but he could handle pain over constant waves of nausea and dizziness.

Drip.

Drip.

Drip.

His eyelids became heavier. Slowly, even the pain began to melt away.

Drip.

Drip.

Drip.

He could rest a moment. Five more minutes wasn't going to make a difference.

Drip.

Drip.

Drip.

CHAPTER 9

S eth woke up with a huge gasp. He was still lying in the hospital bed, but was now in a different room, on one the wards, which he shared with three other patients who were all quietly enjoying their dinner in bed. Seth's injured hand was neatly bandaged with clean dressings.

How long have I been asleep? Oh god, what time is it?

The clock on the wall read 18:35 PM. He'd lost half a day. His whole body broke out in a fine sweat as adrenaline surged and panic set in. Worse than the panic was the ache in his lower abdomen, but it wasn't coming from his groin. His bladder was about to explode.

The bag of fluids hanging on the IV stand beside his bed was crumpled in on itself as the last few drops travelled down the line to his arm.

He pushed the call bell and waited.

His bladder spasmed and he knew there wasn't

time to wait patiently for the nurse to come discon-
nect him from the IV line. He twisted the end of the
line where it connected to the cannula in his arm and
tossed it aside. Seth raced for the hallway, nearly
colliding with a nurse carrying a cardboard kidney
dish full of medicines.

"Watch where you're going," the nurse snapped
at him.

He grabbed hold of her shirt to catch his balance,
and stared at her wide eyed like a crazy person.

"Where's the bathroom?" he asked.

She pointed toward the end of the hallway.
"Over there."

"Thank you."

Seth sprinted for the door marked with stick
figures of a man and lady standing beside each other.

"Security!" the nurse called once there was
enough distance between the two of them. She
dashed off in the opposite direction toward the
nurses' station. "Security!"

"Fuck me," Seth shook his head in disbelief as he
tried to turn the handle on the door and discovered it
was locked from the inside.

An old lady's voice replied from behind the locked
door. "Just a minute."

Even the sounds of her moving inside where at a
glacial pace.

The lid of the toilet seat closed.

Pause.

Urine started tinkling in the toilet bowl.

Pause.

Another few drops of urine.

Longer pause.

Seth knocked on the door again. "Please hurry."

"You'll have to be patient, young man. I said I would only be a minute."

"More like five," he muttered under his breath.

Seth folded his arms and leaned back against the door. Another spasm of his bladder. He was literally about to explode.

"Please, it's an emergency," he said, almost in tears.

The old lady inside the bathroom huffed. "Well, why don't you use the one that's down the hallway. This one is occupied."

Before his mind had engaged, his legs were carrying him down the hallway, and his eyes were scanning every door he passed for one of those little stick men. He was nearing the end of the hallway, and about to turn back, when out the corner of his eye he saw the word *STAFF* on one of the doors.

He skidded to a halt and burst through the door into the staff bathroom. There was a row of lockers and a single stall at the far end of the room that was empty. Seth's fingers fumbled trying to unbutton his jeans as he raced for the finish line. He made it, feet positioned either side of the toilet, back arched ready for release, and reached into his jeans to pull out his...

...his hand touched moist stitches running in a line from his pubic bone to his perineum.

He looked down at the toilet bowl and his face crumpled. His jeans dropped to his knees and he spun around where he was standing to sit down on the toilet seat.

It was wet with small puddles of urine.

Who the fuck pissed on the toilet seat?

As if Seth had never taken a piss without lifting up the seat first. He tried to relax and let the urine flow, but he couldn't. He'd gone past the point where he had control of his bladder.

Relax, Seth.

But something else was preventing him from going. He looked down at the scabbed gash between his legs.

"Oh my god, it hurts so bad."

He leaned forward and bore down at hard as he could. A clot dislodged and urine sprayed from what was left of his urethra, splashing onto his backside and gushing down to fill the bowl with rose tinged beer colored piss. But as the torrential relief slowed to a trickle, the salty sting became a singeing burn between his legs.

He scrunched a few pieces of toilet paper together and pressed them against his gash. The paper slipped through his trembling fingers into the toilet bowl. With his head in his hands, he sat and tried to quash the sense of shame, of emasculation, of the unbearable pain that he'd brought upon himself by some careless action in his past.

What did I do to deserve this?

He couldn't fathom any act of omission or commission in his life that would warrant such harsh, cruel and unfair punishment.

Ring, ring, ring, ring, bananaphone — the chipmunk sang from the phone in his pocket.

"555-0135 calling"

"Fuck," Seth cursed out loud.

He answered the call.

"I'm proud of you, Seth," said the modulated voice. He had no fucking clue what the voice was talking about. "You've done well. Have you seen the evening news?"

"No, I have not," he said coldly.

"Where are you?"

About an inch from snapping your neck!

He caught himself about to say his thoughts out loud.

"At a hospital, somewhere in the city."

"Were you taking the pills I gave you?"

"Yes."

The voice sighed.

"You're running out of time, Seth. I hope you didn't tell them about us?"

As if the modulated voice needed to keep repeating the same mantra of urgency. But he wasn't going anywhere fast without his wheels. And how was he supposed to pay for his stay in hospital? That was a problem for later, and he promised himself he'd come back and pay every penny he owed. For now, he didn't have any more time to waste. He didn't have the luxury of time to stop and explain himself. If he didn't have his wallet on him for them to be able to identify him when he got to the hospital, he must have left it in his car when he went into the drug store.

"I need to get my car, and swing by my house—"

"I wouldn't do that if I were you."

"Why?"

"If I told you it would spoil the surprise. Why don't you go online and see for yourself?"

Seth lost his cool. He'd been teetering on the edge of tipping point, and her not so funny games had pissed him right off. He ended the call before he said something he might regret.

One more wipe, a new sanitary pad from the shelf beside the toilet, jeans back on, hands washed, and he was back in the hallway. The nurse was waiting with two security guards outside the nurses' station.

"There he is," she screamed and pointed in Seth's direction.

The security guards' hands went to the tasers at their sides as they started to run in his direction. Seth bolted for the elevator at the end of the hallway. There was a sign for the stairs, and an arrow pointing through a door beside the elevators. That would have to be his backup if the elevator didn't open in time.

For once, luck was on his side. The doors opened with a *bing* just as he reached for the button. A man carrying a bouquet of flowers stepped out with a smile on his face.

"Sir, stop!" shouted one of the security guards.

Seth slipped past the man carrying the flowers and entered the elevator. He didn't look back, he simply hit the button for the ground floor and slumped against the mirrored wall. The security guards were too slow, and the doors closed long before they caught up. Lights illuminated the number of each floor as the elevator descended. As he approached the ground floor, Seth's anxiety began to rise.

The elevator doors opened with another *bing*. There was no cavalry waiting to arrest him, no one with weapons drawn and trained on his every move. Instead, patients and visitors milled about like zombies in the busy entranceway. Seth quickly slipped through the crowd toward the front doors.

"Have a good day," said the smiling security guard at the entrance.

Seth turned and looked at him in surprise, nodded his head. He noticed a faint buzz of static coming from the guard's waist where his two-way radio was attached to his belt. Seth was certain he could hear, ever so quietly, the words "... *I repeat, the man is dressed in jeans and a black hoodie. Heading your way. Please acknowledge...".*

Seth walked to the nearest taxi and climbed in.

"Where you headed?" asked the driver.

Seth opened the Maps app and looked up the last address he'd searched for, the drug store.

"Can you take me here?"

He showed the driver the map.

"Sure, bud. That's not far from here."

As the taxi pulled into traffic, Seth breathed a sigh of relief, but something told him this was only the calm before the storm. If what the psycho had said was true, then things were about to get real.

He opened the browser on the phone and logged in to his Facebook account.

That's odd, thirty-seven unread messages and a hundred and fifty-one notifications?

The color drained from his face and he could have sworn his heart stopped beating for a few seconds.

What the fuck have I done?

His newsfeed was awash with posts of sheer disbelief, photos and clips from the video he'd leaked to the local newspaper.

— *Oh my GOD! Kerry Jones was ACTUALLY raped!*

— *WTF I used to date one of those assholes.*

— I can't believe it! Bring back the death penalty for rapists.

— Kerry Jones killed herself because of those animals.

He'd been tagged in over seventy posts, along with hundreds of other young people who'd been at the party that night. Everyone was in total shock and outraged, begging for blood to be spilled. Photos of the guys who'd participated were splashed all throughout his newsfeed with "*RAPIST*" stamped across their foreheads, shared and shared, again and again.

Seth was scared to look at his messages.

"You okay back there?" asked the driver. "You look like you've just seen a ghost."

"I'm..." Seth cleared his throat. "Are we almost there?"

"A couple more blocks."

Seth didn't need to read the messages in full to know what they were about. Group messages between his friends sharing their complete horror at what they'd just seen, what Kerry Jones must have gone through in the aftermath that led her to suicide, and what was going to happen to the guys who were responsible. These young men had been their boyfriends, their friends, their bullies, their idols, they were all guys who everyone looked up to, who parents wished their sons could be. Not any more.

At least no one was debating the authenticity of the video.

He opened a chain of messages from his mom. They started with the ones from last night. It seemed so long ago, when he thought he was going for the hookup of a lifetime.

— *Seth answer your phone. It's almost midnight. You were meant to be back from your date by 11.*

— *Seth, where are you? I've tried calling you a hundred times. I'm really worried. Why aren't you answering your phone?*

— *You'd better be using condoms. I'm too young to be a grandmother.*

— *You're grounded.*

He did a double take when he came across a reply from himself to his mom. His mutilator must have sent it.

Chill, mom. I got a flat tire. Mikey rescued me and I stayed at his place. I didn't want to wake you guys up in the middle of the night. —

His mom had replied with a happy face.

— :-)

— I'm so glad you're talking to Mikey again. How are his parents? I was so worried.

The next message was sent less than twenty minutes ago.

— Have you seen the news? The police arrested boys from your college for raping that girl! One of them was Mikey!!!! Are you alright?

— Oh my god I just watched the video. Did you know

*anything about this? You took that girl upstairs! Please tell
me you didn't do anything stupid.*

*— Why aren't you answering your phone. I'm trying
to call.*

*— The police are here and they want to talk to you. They
won't tell me anything. I'm so scared. Come home Seth.
Please answer your phone.*

He scrolled through the other messages, all the same
thing repeated over and over; shock, horror, disbelief.
Then he came upon a message from Mikey.

— WTF, Seth! WHAT HAVE YOU DONE?!!!!!

There was a voice message attached.

"What have you done, Seth? The fucking cops are
standing outside my front door!" Mikey starts hyper-
ventilating and whining. "You broke into my fucking
house? Why the fuck, man? I thought we were
friends? I'm on that video. They're calling us rapists. I

didn't rape anyone. She wanted it." He sobs for a few seconds. In the background, Seth can hear Mikey's mom knocking on the door.

"Mikey, please come out. The police want to talk to you about something," his mom says, her voice warbling

"I'm coming now, Mom," he shouted back. Mikey spoke softly. "If I ever see you again, you're fucking dead! Do you hear me?"

The message ended.

Seth glanced up to see the taxi driver staring at him in the rearview mirror.

"What did you do, bro?" asked the driver. "He sounded pissed at you."

"Never mind," said Seth.

"We're here now," said the driver as he pulled the cab up to the sidewalk outside the drug store.

"How much do I owe you?"

"Eight bucks fifty."

"Can you wait a minute while I get the money from my car?"

The driver spun around in his seat to scowl at Seth.

"You trying to rip me off, bro?"

"No, I'm good for it," Seth said as he climbed out the car and walked across the street to where he was parked.

The taxi driver watched him with a steely gaze. Seth opened his door — the keys were still in the ignition — and pulled his wallet out of the glove box. He walked back to the cab and handed over the cash.

"Hey, don't do anything crazy," said the driver.

"Sure," said Seth. "Thanks for the ride."

The cab driver wound up the window and drove away.

Ring, ring, ring, ring, bananaphone — the chipmunk sang from the phone in his pocket.

"555-0135 calling"

Seth answered the call as he got behind the wheel of his car. He put the loudspeaker on and dropped the phone into the cup holder.

"Hello," Seth said, turning the key in the ignition.

"I see you're moving again," said the modulated voice.

They're tracking me. How did I not realize this before?

Seth picked up the phone and flicked through the settings. He scrutinized the list of apps running in the background and couldn't see anything out of the ordinary.

"Are you there, Seth?"

He realized he hadn't said anything for the last half a minute.

"I'm here."

"You've completed your first task and brought justice. Now you must show that you can do something honorable."

"What do you want me to do?"

"There's a girl. Her name's Catherine Holmes. You called her Kitty Cat. Do the right thing, Seth, and you'll be another step closer to getting your precious dick back."

The phone call ended.

Catherine Holmes? Was she a girl I hooked up with at the beginning of sophomore year?

He couldn't even visualize what she looked like, only her name. But he knew he could easily track her down online. They must have had friends of friends if they knew each other from before?

He thought he'd try Facebook first. That had to be a good bet. But he got no hits that resembled any girl he'd ever known by the name of Catherine Holmes.

She's probably using her middle name as her last name. It's what everyone's doing these days for privacy.

That was a dead end from the start. He could run through every possible name he could think of, and still not guess right.

Hopelessness began to fester, and the knot in Seth's stomach started twisting itself even tighter.

He was all out of ideas.

Seth picked up the phone with every intention of admitting defeat. He pictured his big cock and balls falling into the waste disposal and instantly being ground up into a fine mince. Thank god he never waited for marriage like his mother always wanted him to. What a crock of shit! Same reason why you shouldn't work like a slave, live like a pauper, save every penny and sacrifice happiness, aiming to cash it all in at retirement. What if he got hit by a bus? What if he got cancer? It would have all been an epic waste of a life. At least he never wasted his dick while it was still good to him.

Seth picked up the phone and starting writing a text message to his tormentor.

Help —

Seconds later he received a reply.

— *What's wrong?*

The grumbling rage bubbled up again. Seth was finding it harder to control the urge to lash out at everything around him.

How do I find Catherine Holmes? —

— :-)

— *I can help with that.*

Another brief pause.

— *2b/65 Monterey Drive*

He hesitated and took a few deep breaths.

Thank you —

— *My pleasure :-)*

— *Are you taking your pills?*

No. He hadn't even thought about the pills since the drug store. The doctor had loaded him up in hospital with antibiotics and he wasn't getting the sweaty shakes anymore... for now.

Which is which again? —

— *Blue = painkiller = 4 hrs*

— *White = antibiotic = 6 hrs*

— *Got it?*

Got it —

What was the time? Was he due another pill yet? He had no idea but he'd started with ten pills and he had four left. Three blue and one white.

Couldn't hurt to take one anyway, right?

The last white pill went down his gullet, followed by a blue one.

He stared at the remaining two blue pills. He was still in so much pain, and wanted so desperately for it all to end. Another blue pill went into his mouth and he swallowed.

Seth tapped on the address and a map opened with directions to Monterey Drive from his current location. He was only a couple of miles away.

Every minute of the drive there, his mind kept running through the scenarios of what happened during those lost hours in the motel room. Had he been raped, too? Was that another lesson he had to learn on top of the mutilation? It was something he hadn't wanted to deal with at the time and suppressed. But how else could he explain the lube all over his ass and the screaming agony that accompanied taking a dump this morning? He should have been angry. He should have felt something. But Seth's emotions were deadened, all used up, running on empty.

As he turned down one suburban street after the next, he began to get a sense of déjà vu, a vague recollection of this part of town like he'd been here before. He turned another street corner as he approached the address and knew exactly where he was.

Catherine Holmes — the first girl he had true feelings for, the girl he epically fucked things up with that night in the back seat of his car.

An overwhelming dread washed over Seth. This wasn't about to go well.

CHAPTER 10

2 Years Earlier

Everything about the girl made Seth hard with desire. They'd met on the lawns outside the Law Faculty, friends of friends, and hit it off immediately. He called her Kitty Cat but her real name was Catherine. She seemed to like the term of endearment, giggled whenever he used it around her. He wasn't trying to be sweet and romantic, like any other guy his age he was desperate to get in her pants and the quickest route to the highway of heaven was through sweet nothings and affection. It wasn't rocket science. The formula was simple:

(Girls) Hugs and kisses = sexy times (Guys)

His friends teased him about asking her out on a date. Mikey especially. Mikey had known Cat since high school days and she'd never shown any interest in him. For once, Seth wasn't competing with his best friend for a girl's attention, he'd won without even trying.

Things had gone better than planned. By the end of that first afternoon together they'd kissed behind the library. Second day they kissed in his car after he dropped her off at home. For their first official date they went to the movies where they sat in the back row and kissed all the way through. At one point, she lay her hand on his thigh and — mistakenly — landed on the rigid swelling in his pants. She let her hand linger for at least a minute while Seth sat pinned to his seat like a mesmerized cobra under the spell of a snake charmer.

As the credits began to roll, she whispered in his ear, "Is there somewhere we can go?"

International language for *I want you to fuck my brains out.*

Seth knew just the spot.

He'd taken a few girls there just recently, the ones who were too nervous to go back to his apartment. As if going with a stranger deep into the industrial area of town at night was any less dangerous. Not that he had any ill intentions.

This particular spot was located in a business park car lot, which during the day was gridlocked with vehicles and commuters, but at night you could hear crickets. Metaphorically, of course, because everything was concreted and there wasn't a square inch of grass for miles.

Developments like this had been popping up all around the outskirts of town, drawing business, mostly IT firms from the expensive rents in the central city to cheaper, shiny new buildings. The nearest residential area was a five minute drive away. Seth knew they'd be uninterrupted.

In the car ride on the way there, they made superficial chit chat about the movie, which neither of them had paid much attention to. Kitty Cat was nervous, but Seth had done this a thousand times before. He'd already rehearsed a hundred times in his head how he was going to devour her in the back seat of his car. It seldom worked out the way he planned, too many variables, and that was the fun of a fantasy — he never knew how it would play out in real life. But it never failed to get his engine revving and ready to go.

He parked the car and they climbed onto the back seat where there was more space.

She was keen — super keen — running her hands across his muscled pecs, and six pack abs.

"I want you so bad," said Seth.

"You too."

They attacked each other's lips with passionate kisses. Seth lay down on top of Cat and she wrapped her legs around his waist.

"I want to make love to you," said Seth.

Love? Lol. Fuck her brains out, more like it.

"My dad is expecting me home by eleven."

"Mine, too. We'll be quick."

She said nothing as he nuzzled her neck and explored her breasts with tiny kisses.

"Okay,"

"You sure? We can wait if you're not ready."

No girl in the history of his conquests had ever said no after he pulled that line on them.

She nodded her head and stared at him, mildly terrified, her body trembling with excitement. He kissed her and she gave her body over to him.

Like the expert Casanova he was, Seth managed to unbutton his jeans and pull off her panties without breaking their passionate kiss for even a second.

He pressed himself against her mound. She was already wet with anticipation. She wanted him so badly, he could tell.

Suddenly, her body tensed and she brought her hand between their lips.

"Wait, wait, wait," she said with urgency. "What about a condom?"

"It's okay," he hushed her with a finger to her lips. "Let me feel you. Just for a minute, and then I'll pull out."

It's not that Seth had deliberately forgotten to bring a condom. He had a supply sitting in his glove box, hidden behind his emergency breakdown kit so his mom wouldn't find them. But he wanted to test the waters with this girl. See how far was she was willing to let him go. And right then he was about an inch over the finishing line.

Her body relaxed and he lowered himself till their pubic bones touched. She quivered, as they always did when he was fully inside them, and her lips parted to release a small whimper. He often wondered what it was like for the girls when he entered them. As a man it was a mystery he would never know the answer to.

They kissed and he rocked his hips back and forth. She clutched at his ass cheeks, running her fingers through the light layer of fuzz, and pulling him deeper, further, harder into her.

Oh my god, she feels incredible.

Seth stared into her eyes and saw something he'd never seen before. The way she was gazing back at him. Was it love? It was more than lust. And somewhere deep down he knew he felt the same way about her. She was the girl, the one he could see himself bringing home to Mom and Dad, getting down on one knee and proposing on a romantic weekend away in the mountains, making love in front of the fire, and bringing babies into the world.

"I think I lo..." Seth began to say the words he'd never said to any girl before Kitty Cat, but suddenly stopped. "Oh shit, no. I think I'm about to..." Seth shouted out loud.

Catherine would have jumped two feet in the air had his body not been pinning her down.

The moment arrived too soon. Seth pulled out as

quickly as he could, but he was mid ejaculation, half of which he'd deposited inside her vault, the rest flew through the air and covered her brand new pretty pink shirt that she'd worn specially for their date.

"Stop, stop," screamed Catherine. "Get off me!"

"I'm so sorry," said Seth, dabbing at the mess on her shirt, smearing it in bigger wet patches.

Catherine squirmed out from under him.

"Don't touch it!" she screamed.

"I'm sure I pulled out in time."

But even Seth didn't believe his own lie.

Catherine pulled a couple of tissues out the back pocket of her pants and wiped between her legs, trying to mop up the mess.

Her distress turned to fury as she looked down at the wet tissues.

"You fucking idiot!" she screamed at Seth, throwing the wad at him.

He turned away and the tissues hit the side of his face, sticking to his stubble. Seth was stunned into horrified silence.

"Eww, gross," said Seth as he swatted the tissues off his face with the tips of his fingers, trying not to touch it.

"Gross? I have that inside me!"

"It's okay, it'll be okay," said Seth, hands in the air, trying to calm her.

Catherine fought him off, kicking and screaming.

"Get away from me!"

Seth could see that he needed to give her space.

He climbed out the car and slammed the door closed behind him.

"Fuck!" he yelled into the quiet night. His voice echoed back at him from the surrounding buildings.

Catherine climbed through to the passenger seat and sat with her head in her hands, sobbing.

"What do I do?" he asked himself over and over. He turned away from the car, too embarrassed to show his face.

A car door opened.

"Get... IN... THE CAR!" Catherine said, each word angrier than the last.

Seth spun around just as Catherine sat down again in the passenger seat. He made his way back to the car and climbed in. She had her arms folded across her chest, staring ahead, ignoring Seth.

"I'm so sorr—"

She cut him off with a sharp, "Shh!"

"Just shut up and start the car," ordered Catherine.

He did as he was told.

"What you're going to do now is drive us to the nearest drug store. You're going to go in and explain what you have done. Because I obviously can't go in with a money shot all over my chest. You're going to get me the morning after pill. Then you're going to take me home and explain to my parents why their little girl is in tears."

Seth sat in his seat, shell shocked.

"Drive, Seth."

He started the car and drove in a daze.

A few minutes later, they were outside the drug store. He went in and returned with the pill in a small brown paper bag. He handed it to Catherine, who took it without looking at him or saying a word. For some reason, he'd expected a thank you, but realized it was probably the last thing he deserved.

They drove back to Catherine's house in silence. She stared out the window the entire journey, a blank expression on her face, tears pooled in the corners of her eyes, but no other outward emotion.

Seth wanted to ask what she was thinking. He got close to plucking up the courage to speak but swallowed it down again. They turned onto Monterey Drive and Catherine reached down to her feet to collect her things that were sitting on the floor.

"You ready to face the music?" she asked Seth.

Did she seriously think it was a good idea for him to tell her parents about their... accident?

That's fucked up. Why the hell do they need to know?

Catherine inhaled deeply, and then slowly blew out all her breath.

"Are you ready?" she turned to Seth.

He nodded.

They both opened their car doors at the same time. Catherine got out and faced the house.

There was a squeal of tires and roar from the engine as Seth took off at high speed down the street.

Catherine ran out into the road, hands in the air. Seth tilted his rearview mirror up so he didn't have to watch her as he drove away.

The adrenaline was making his head spin. He switched on the radio to the loudest heavy metal he could find and screamed along to the angry lyrics.

"Holy shit, that was intense." He shook out his entire body and breathed the longest sigh of relief. "Who the fuck tells their parents? That's fucked up, man!"

What he needed was some weed to chill out and celebrate escaping the clutches of that psycho bitch.

What's Mikey up to? I'll send him a text.

So what if he'd prematurely ejaculated in her snatch? It's not like he was obliged to get married to her. He justified his decision to leave her at the curb in a hundred different ways.

What did she think would happen if they started fucking without a condom? She went into it with eyes wide open.

What if she had this planned all along?

Psycho fucking bitch!

CHAPTER 11

Present Day

S eth walked up to the front door of 2b/65
Monterey Drive. It was a shitty unit down a
shared lane, a few houses from where
Catherine used to live with her parents. There was
washing hanging on the line outside which was cast
in shadows. Nothing would ever dry in a damp,
murky place like that.

He knocked on the door, half hoping no one
would answer.

"Just a second," a young woman called out from
inside.

A pretty brunette girl opened the door with a
smile, which instantly melted into a cold stare.

"Hello, Seth," said Catherine. "What do
you want?"

Her anger toward him hadn't diminished since he last saw her.

"I came because... " Though he had no idea why he'd been made to go there. "I... I... "

Catherine looked at her wristwatch.

"Just spit it out, Seth. It's getting late and I have things to do."

"I owe you an apology."

She burst into a fit of giggles.

"W-why are you laughing?"

"Seriously? I don't want your apologies, Seth. It's too late for that."

She stared him up and down.

"Look, whatever crisis you're going through at the moment, I'm sorry, but I'm not interested in helping. You're on your own."

She started to turn away and push the door closed. Seth wedged his foot in the door.

"Wait, wait," he said.

"What are you doing? Get out of my house," said Catherine.

There was a pitter patter of small feet, and a kid around two years old ran up behind Catherine. He had sandy blond hair, and big bright blue eyes, the spitting image of Seth as a toddler.

"Mommy, come," said the boy.

Catherine shielded him behind her legs.

"I'm coming now," she said.

She turned to Seth and spoke sternly. "I'd like you to leave."

"Is that?" he said in disbelief.

"Please don't do this to us," she begged, the thunder cloud above her head vanished and all that remained was distress.

"I'm not here to upset you," he said, trying to reassure her.

"Then what are you here for?"

"Who that?" asked the little boy. He pushed past his mother's legs to get a better look at the man standing at the door. "Me Ben. Me big boy," he said to Seth with the proudest smile.

Seth's heart melted with love for the child he'd never known.

"Hey, little man," said Seth, getting down on his haunches to greet the boy at eye level. He grinned through the pain in what was once his crotch.

"That's enough," said Catherine, brushing Ben back inside the house. "I think you should leave."

She turned to Ben. "Bubba, go fetch your books. I'm coming to read to you now."

Ben's face brimmed with excitement. He raced back into the house.

Seth had so many questions he wanted to ask.

I have a child. I'm a... father.

"Spit it out, Seth."

He said nothing.

"You want to know why I didn't take the pill. Well, I did. It didn't work. But I knew it wouldn't be worth the effort telling you. Look at you. Are you on drugs?"

"No, no... I... I'll make it up to you."

A sudden calm came over Catherine. "You don't get it, do you? I don't want you to be a part of his life."

"I don't think I deserve that."

"At least we agree on something."

Seth fidgeted with his hands. He had to use every bit of emotional strength left to stop himself from crying.

"You know what you're feeling right now?" said Catherine. "Guilt. It's coming in waves isn't it? Like the worst nausea ever? Throat like it's about to close up so tight you can hardly breathe?" She nodded and glared at him. "Imagine how I felt when the doctors told me I was pregnant and it was too late to have an abortion?" She pointed an index finger at him and prodded his chest. "Imagine how it felt when I told my parents I was pregnant, and my father screamed at me for an hour, and didn't speak to me for a month." The tears streamed down her cheeks. "Imagine what it was like to drop out of college, give up my dreams, and take the first receptionist job I could find before my baby bump grew big enough to give away that I was pregnant and unemployable."

She clutched her face in her hands, sniffed and rubbed her runny nose.

"Imagine how much strength it took for me to come to you, after all my options had run out, to ask if you would like to be a part of your child's life?"

Wait? What? When did that happen?

Seth stared at her, baffled.

She chuckled. "You don't even remember, do you?"

He shook his head, no idea what she was talking about.

"I blamed it on morning sickness, but I'm sure that it was the thought of having to come to you in such a vulnerable state that made me ill. It took a whole morning for me to pluck up the courage to catch the bus to the university and wait for you to come out of class. Do you know what you said to me when I tried to wave you down?"

He shook his head again, no recollection of any part of what she was telling him.

"In front of everyone." She paused. "You said, 'Hey, how's bareback Barbie doing today?' I was so mortified I stood there speechless with my mouth hanging open. Your friend asked if that was the same expression I had on my face when I blew you."

Seth wanted to vomit. He vaguely remembered what happened that day, of feeling ashamed to see the girl he'd been a dick to a few months earlier waiting to confront him outside class. Rather than lose face in front of his bros, he chose to take the offensive and attack before she could say anything that would make him look bad.

What had been just another offhand insult to look cool in front of his douchebag friends had destroyed a sweet girl's reputation. And not just any girl, but the future mother of his child. If only he had known. If only he hadn't been such an epic asshole.

"Please? I have to make this right." Seth begged.

"Who are you doing this for? Yourself? Or Ben? The biggest investment you could possibly make in *my* son's life is walking away."

The phone in Seth's pocket started tweeting like a tiny bird — *Tweet tweet, tweet tweet.* He ignored it.

"I have a trust. When I turn twenty-one in two month's time I get access to it. It's about a hundred grand. Not a huge amount, but it could go toward his education. Give him a head start in life."

"We don't need your money."

"Please. I have to do something, but I don't know what to do."

"Mommy, come." Ben was standing in the background, cuddling a snuggly blanket decorated with animated cars.

"I'm sorry this isn't what you hoped it would be," said Catherine.

Seth was panicking. Whatever his tormentor had hoped for him to achieve by showing up at the door of an old flame and their secret offspring, he'd failed at miserably.

He put a hand on the door to hold it open.

"Please," he dropped his head in shame and cried.

A few moments later, arms wrapped around him. It was Catherine. He buried his head in her shoulder and bawled his eyes out while they gently rocked together. Her hair smelled of almonds and honey, and it brought him back to that moment when he was lost in rapture, making passionate love to her in the back seat of his car.

There was a tug at his leg as Ben joined the group hug.

"There, there," said Ben, rubbing the back of Seth's thigh.

"I don't take back a single thing that I said. I don't want you in Ben's life. I've got a lovely fiancé, who is an amazing father to Ben. It took a long time, but I'm happy now. "

Catherine stood back and looked at Seth. Her eyes were bloodshot, but she'd managed to hold back the tears.

"Don't make the same mistake again, Seth. Come on, Benny boy," she said, taking Ben by the hand back inside the house.

Ben peered over his shoulder and gave Seth a cute wave as the front door to the tiny unit closed behind them.

Seth traipsed back to the car, body and mind defeated. 'A mistake' — that's what his mother had called Seth. His parents never wanted a baby. He just *happened,* and they had to deal with the fallout. Of course, his mom always said she loved him, every bit of the way, but he came at the worst time for them financially, and put a major dampener on his parents' relationship; emotionally and sexually. His dad never really forgave him for ruining that. And when his mom got pregnant for the second time, it was the end of any kind of connection between his parents. Mom lost the baby and neither of them seemed to care. One day it was there. The next it was gone. One day he was going to be an older brother. The next it was business as usual and they were back to being the same dysfunctional family.

But seeing his beautiful little boy cuddling a blanket, Seth realized how big a fuck up he'd made. He'd broken something that could never be mended, and he would have to live with that knowledge for the rest of his life.

The phone in his pocket tweeted again — *Tweet tweet, tweet tweet.*

How was it all connected, and why make him confront his past? He was supposed to have done something honorable, but all he'd done was upset Catherine, who seemed to be doing just fine before he showed up.

"Seth, wait," Catherine called out as she ran up the lane after him.

He stopped walking and she caught up.

"I'm sorry," she said. "I've been so angry at you for so long. You have no idea the things I've wanted to say to you." She sobbed and brought a hand to cover her mouth. "But I can't keep hating you. I need to move on with my life."

"O-okay." He wasn't sure what to say.

She wiped her eyes and stood up straight again. "This is how it's going to work. When, and only when, you've got your shit sorted out — because I don't want you to be a bad influence on our child — you can contact me again, and we'll arrange something. I don't want your money. But I don't want to lie to Ben about who his father is."

"Of course," said Seth.

Catherine sniffed. "That's all I had to say."

At a total loss for words, Seth nodded solemnly as Catherine turned and headed back to her unit.

Seth climbed back into his car. There were no more pain killers left to dampen the throb in his groin, or the stabbing pain in his head. He shut his eyes and slowed his breathing, trying to will away the pain.

The phone in his pocket tweeted again — *Tweet tweet, tweet tweet.*

He pulled it out and saw three new messages.

— Call me when you can?

— Happy father's day! :-)

— Did u get my last text?

Furious, he called the number back. As soon as the call was answered he didn't wait for a voice to speak.

"How did you know? About Ben? What kind of

sick joke is this? Including innocent children in the mess you've created? You're fucking sick in the head!"

"I'm sorry, Seth. I don't think you have the right to judge me. And we had an agreement. If you were rude to me again, then I would turn one of your balls to mince. Unfortunately, you have forced my hand." A loud grinding noise deafened the ear he had to the phone. Acid wash rose in Seth's throat as the realization came to him that he was one jewel down with only two to go.

As always, the call ended abruptly..

Once the burn in the back of his throat had subsided, he felt nothing, then numbness, and then a cold shiver.

Fuck it, only need one ball, anyway.

He couldn't believe how little he cared, but that psycho was holding all the strings and he had no control over what was going to eventuate. He needed to get it off his chest. In a way, the price he paid for telling his tormentor how he felt was worth it.

He flipped the visor down and stared at his reflection in the mirror. He was ghostly pale with heavy bags under his bloodshot eyes. Sicker than before.

I look like shit.

Another rigor made his body quake, and he broke out in a sweat. The infection was coming back with a vengeance. Whatever they'd given him in the hospital was wearing off quickly, but he had one last task and this whole nightmare would be over.

It was fast turning into one of the coldest nights in weeks, a light mist settling over the city. Seth turned up the heating in the car and rubbed his hands together. He had nothing warmer than the clothes he was wearing.

The phone started ringing. Seth laughed when he saw the same number appear on the screen.

"Asshole can't get enough, can they?"

He tapped on the loudspeaker button.

"What can I do you for?" he said, loud and cheery.

His tone seemed to take his caller by surprise.

"You there?" said Seth.

"I'm disappointed in you, Seth," said the modulated voice. "The way you spoke to me was uncalled for."

"I'm so sorry. I don't know what came over me," he said, almost taunting in his politeness.

"Hmm, apology accepted. It's time for your last task, your chance to do something brave. You have an hour to get to the place where Steve Lewis died. A woman's life depends on it. I believe you know the location well."

The call ended.

The place Steve Lewis died? That didn't make any sense. Everyone knew he died in the ambulance on the way to the hospital after a drug overdose, or did they mean the place where he used to deal from? That had to be it.

Steve Lewis was something of a legend on campus, until he got caught dealing dope and *E* from his frat house. His life basically spiraled out of control and he ended up living homeless in one of the abandoned slaughterhouses down the wrong side of town. Rumor had it he owed a drug cartel a couple of hundred grand when he got bust by campus security. They made him pay for it in ways none of us wanted to imagine, but frequently liked to talk about.

Didn't stop all the college kids from continuing to buy from him though. It was an adventure to go cruising down the mean streets, past the tranny hookers, homeless people, and low lifes who called that part of town home. The ultimate thrill for a rich kid to go slumming it with the poor folk, seeking out their next hit.

Last time Seth saw Steve Lewis alive, Steve was missing his top row of teeth, had lost so much weight his ribs were sticking through his threadbare cotton wife beater, and his eyes were sunken deep in his skull. In the fluorescent lighting, Steve's skin was mildly jaundiced, and his hands trembled like a tweaker in desperate need of another hit.

What a sad way for a high school football hero to go. If only that scholarship he'd won to college had been large enough to cover living expenses, too, things might have ended up different for poor Stevey boy.

Seth started the engine and plugged the address for the old slaughterhouse into the phone.

"29 minutes travel time"

Perfect! He'd get there with time to spare. But what did 'a woman's life depends on it' mean? He was the furthest thing from a hero, and he prayed they weren't expecting him to swoop in and save the day. There were no women in his life important enough that he would risk everything to save them.

A horrific thought entered his mind.

My mom. That psycho has my mom.

Foot flat on the gas, he tore through the quiet suburban streets, ignoring stop signs and streetlights. All he could think about was his mom, and the terrible things that could be happening to her as every second passed by that he wasn't there to save her.

"Please be okay, please," he said out loud.

With one hand on the steering wheel, and the other trying to use the phone, he opened up Facebook and fumbled his way through sending his mom a message.

Mom r u k? —

After a couple of minutes his mom still hadn't replied, adding to the possibility of his worst fears coming true. He checked his phone again as his car passed through a red light, narrowly missing a collision with a cars coming from both his left and his right. One of the drivers stopped in the middle of the intersection, got out and screamed at Seth, flipped him the bird as he sped away.

The miles to his destination slowly dropped to single digits. He had to hurry. If that psycho had done anything to his mom, he was going to make them pay for it, no matter the cost. He didn't care if he lost his own precious body parts for good. None of that mattered if his mom got hurt.

He was almost there now. Past the old rubber factory and then the car scrapyard, toward the overgrown property at the far end of the street that had heavy chains locked around its entrance. His car came to a screeching halt in the mud outside the gates.

Seth threw open his car door and sprinted along the path through the bushes that ran alongside the sixteen foot high barbed wire fencing. He knew exactly where to go, where someone had cut through the fence and folded back a doorway for trespassers to enter.

He had trodden this path many a time when it was his turn to do the weed run for the fraternity. But since Steve's death a few months ago, another dealer had taken his place who dealt from a strip club in town, and there'd been no reason to return to the slaughterhouse.

College kids used to come out here all the time to

do drugs and have parties where no adult would think of looking for them. But now nature had begun to reclaim the path that led down the fence line through the property, to the back entrance where no one could see the visitors coming and going as they pleased.

Someone had walked this path recently, grass freshly pressed down into the mud with footprints and the markings from something heavy being dragged this way.

Stinging nettles clung to Seth's jeans as he waded through the thick undergrowth. Smoke was coming out one of the slaughterhouse chimneys, and he could hear the hum of a generator. Somewhere inside the building a saw was roaring violently.

"Mom!" Seth yelled as he tried to run as fast as he could toward the back entrance. It was more of a hop and a hobble as pain tore into his groin like a fresh wound was being slashed between his legs with every stride.

"I'm coming, Mom!"

The back entrance was open, and the sounds of the inner workings of the slaughterhouse in motion led him into the bowels of the facility. It was dark as night inside the slaughterhouse, musky from years of black mold growing unabated on every surface. He ran out onto the kill floor and jumped with fright as the rows of meat hooks hanging from the ceiling began to shake and move in a uniform line toward the bleeding area.

"Mom? Where are you?"

The few unbroken fluorescent lights that remained flickered to life on the ceiling high above him. They flickered like strobe lights in a nightclub, none of them achieving a solid white glow. The space became claustrophobic as his eyes were no longer able to adjust further than a few feet in front of him between flashes of the lights.

A hook swung in front of his face, nearly impaling his eye. Seth fell back onto the floor, grazing his hands on the rough concrete. This time, something ripped for sure between his legs. He clutched his groin, doubled over in agony.

The noises within the slaughterhouse grew as other parts of the production line came to life: cables groaned, gears ground, and saws whirred. Seth put his hands on his knees and forced himself back up to a standing position. The sounds were overwhelming his senses. Blinded by the constant strobing lights he quickly became disoriented, wandering lost in the dark.

All of a sudden there was silence as the power went out and the machinery switched off. Seth was left with a deafening, high pitched ringing in his ears. His pupils quickly adjusted to the dark again. Somewhere, beyond all the noise, someone had been screaming. A woman. He could hear her now. Her terrified cries left Seth cold.

"Mom?!"

"Help me," he heard the woman's cries echoing

from deeper inside the slaughterhouse. "Please, hurry!"

It wasn't his mother's voice, he could tell that much. None of this felt right. But his primal instincts spurred him on, drove him forward to find whoever was in trouble and rescue them. This wasn't the old Seth, the selfish young guy who never lifted a finger unless he had something to gain out of his actions. He hardly recognized the man running bravely through the dark to face who knows what lay waiting for him on the other side.

The generator grunted and power returned. The conveyor belt system that ran from room to room began to move, its rusty wheels screeched and groaned.

"Help, I don't want to die down here!" the woman screamed, and then her voice was drowned out by the machinery coming to life again.

There was a light on up ahead, and the horrible whirring sound of a meat bandsaw catching on metal. Seth hobbled as quickly as he could, gritting his teeth to deaden the excruciating pain. The bandsaw grew louder, and so did the woman's cries as he moved close enough to once again hear her.

"Please help me!"

Seth entered the processing floor and for a moment was frozen with fear. There was a young woman, possibly the same age as him, handcuffed to the conveyor belt, rapidly approaching a saw that ran through the center of the conveyor belt. In its working life it would have been what the factory workers used on the production line to cut the pieces of meat up into smaller parts for packing, but now it was about to slice a girl in half.

Seth almost didn't notice a small glass jar moving along another nearby conveyor belt, this one destined for the smoking room ovens. But out the corner of his eye he noticed the vicious flames erupting from the ovens. In the flickering light of their flames he caught a glimpse of what the jar contained; a large bloody penis and half-empty scrotum.

A terrible dilemma of cosmic proportions smacked Seth in the gut. The jar was maybe half a minute away from traveling down the conveyor belt and into the fiery furnace. Even packed with ice, his precious parts wouldn't stand a chance against the intense heat that warmed his skin from where he was standing.

Something came over him. He stopped thinking and ran. There was no thought. There was no pain. Only purpose. He cleared the gap in a couple of seconds and grabbed the girl beneath her armpits. One huge heave and she didn't budge. She was a bigger girl, but that wasn't the problem. She'd been chained by her feet to the rungs of the conveyor belt, a set of handcuffs around each ankle. Her face was grimy and there were marks where tears had streamed down her chubby cheeks and washed away the dirt.

"Oh thank god," she screamed. "Hurry! He threw the key over there! It's somewhere by the door."

Seth looked around. There were three entrances to the room. "Which door?"

"That way," she gestured with her head and hand back over her shoulder toward the opposite side of the room where a smashed Emergency Exit light hung over the door. "Please hurry!"

If he didn't find that key she was as good as dead.

He screamed with rage and ran for the exit door, dropped to his knees and ran his bare hands across the floor surface. Nothing. His heart pounded so hard that every beat was pulsating through his throbbing head.

"I can't find it!"

"You have to!" the girl screamed. "I don't want to die!"

She was edging ever closer to the meat cutting saw.

Then he felt the cold metal outline of a jagged key edge.

"I got it," he yelled with joy and raced back to the girl. "I found the key!"

She was panic-stricken, squirming on the conveyor belt, trying to pull her feet through the handcuffs, bleeding where they dug into her soft squishy flesh. Less than a few feet from the saw, she covered her eyes and cried, giving up all hope of rescue.

Seth fumbled with the key, almost dropping it as he came to a skidding halt beside the girl.

"It's going to be okay. I'll get you out of this."

"I'm gonna die," she broke down completely, bawling her eyes out.

Vibrations from the bandsaw made his hands wobble as he rested his arms on the conveyor belt.

He turned and watched as the glass jar that held his stolen bits was engulfed by flames on the other side of the room. The glass shattered inside the smoker and Seth whimpered like a hurt puppy.

The key slipped into the lock, and with a single turn of the mechanism it opened. Seth grabbed the girl's shirt and yanked her over the edge of the conveyor belt, using his weight for momentum. She still had one leg attached to the conveyor belt, but her body swung freely over the side, out of harm's way.

Her body crushed his chest and left him winded. The conveyor belt groaned as it dragged her away.

"Help," she screamed. "My other leg!"

She tried to walk her body along the ground with her hands, but couldn't keep up the pace. Her upper body collapsed under its own weight and was dragged along the floor.

"Help me!"

Seth sprung back onto his feet and raced behind her. He jumped onto the conveyor belt. The key slid into the lock easily enough, but refused to budge.

"It won't unlock!"

He twisted the key with so much force that when

the lock gave way he thought he'd broken it. The handcuffs clicked open and suddenly her leg was freed. The girl slumped onto the ground, her fore-arms covered in grazes, bleeding in places from rubbing on the rough concrete floor.

She was almost inconsolable.

Seth sat down beside her. He put his arms around her, cradled her shuddering body, and they cried together. It all seemed so surreal, so cruel, so point-less. What sort of monster would do this to another person? There was no way he could have won this test that was rigged from the very start.

"Thank you," said the girl. "I thought I was going to die."

He didn't know what to say to her, simply stared at her stunned eyes and stupefied expression.

An expression he'd seen somewhere before.

She wiped her tears, smearing the grime across her cheeks, and held Seth's hand.

"It's going to be okay, now you're here."

"Did you see who did this to you?" asked Seth.

Her lips trembled and she shook her head.

"You must have seen something? Was he tall? Short? Black? White?"

She just shook her head.

"What do you mean?"

She buried her face in her hands.

"I didn't see him. It was so dark."

"I'm sorry, I didn't mean to... " said Seth, ashamed of himself for grilling her.

He pulled out the phone that was in his pocket. No messages waiting for him to read. Was it really all over?

"Have you called 911? Are they on their way?"

Seth gently shook his head.

"What's the point, he'll be miles away by now." He hung his head, defeated.

"Good," she said. "It's better if we have this time together."

What does she mean by that?

"I always had faith in you," she continued.

"Faith to do what?"

"To rescue me."

The skin on his back began to crawl.

"I just knew that when all hope was lost you would pull through."

She wasn't making any sense at all.

"How long ago did the guy leave? If I run now will I be able to catch him?"

"It's okay, Seth. None of that matters any more."

She put her bloody, dirty hands up to his chin and stared into his eyes.

"You're a better person now."

"What are you talking about?"

"You did it, you chose someone else over your... your penis. You saved me!"

The girl bounced onto her knees and edged closer to Seth. He leaned away from her.

"What did you just say?"

She startled and scooted a few feet away.

"Please don't be angry at me. I only wanted the best for you."

"WHAT?!"

"You don't need your penis. You're perfect without it. Now you'll never have to worry about giving into temptation. We can be happy... in love."

And then the penny dropped. The girl. Her face. That stupefied expression. He knew where he recognized her from. The Valentine's Day party. The girl on the sofa who never said a word while he used her body as a dumping ground for his disappointment.

"You? You did this!" He rose to his feet, a thunderstorm of anger gathered around his head. "Did you plan this whole thing on your own? Or did someone help you?"

The girl cowered behind a pole and slunk further away to the other side of the conveyor belt.

"Did you trick me into going to that motel, cut off my fucking penis and balls... and send me on a wild goose chase? For what? To make me a better fucking person?"

He grew apoplectic with rage, his vision turned shades of black and white as his blood pressure soared.

"It's okay, Seth. I took away the worst part of you. There's nothing left to lead you astray. Your penis was never going to bring you happiness. I can do that. I can make you happy."

He chortled like a mad man. "Why don't you come

over here and I'll show you how happy you've made me?"

She shook her head.

"Why not?" he asked angrily.

"I'm scared. You're angry with me."

"No fucking shit, you psycho bitch! You mutilated me, and now you want to live happily ever after? Are you fucking insane?!"

The girl began to cry. She pressed herself up against the far wall and crawled up into the fetal position.

Seth jumped over the conveyor belt. He saw the switch hanging from the ceiling which controlled the production line and pushed it, bringing the belt to an abrupt stop.

"No! I'm not insane. I'm behaving exactly like any ordinary person would behave after... " he screamed "... after having their fucking dick and balls cut off!"

He reached down and picked her up by the scruff of her neck. She was terrified, scrunching her face up in fear, too afraid to even look at Seth.

"You're pathetic." He spat in her face and threw her onto the ground.

Seth held his head and cried. He tried to think what to do next. His mind kept spiraling out of control trying to make sense of everything.

He made up his mind. "I'm calling the cops."

"I wouldn't do that if I were you," said the girl.

Seth looked up from his phone to see her glaring at him, nostrils flared like a wild animal.

She pulled something out of her pocket. Seth ducked, thinking it might have been a gun.

"Such a pussy! Scared of a girl with a phone in her pocket?" She prowled left and then right. "And you called yourself a man? What are you now? Castrated? A eunuch? Pathetic! That's what you are!"

Seth watched her in stunned disbelief.

She tapped her phone and held the screen up for him to see.

"Who's the bitch now?"

He only saw a glimpse of the screen before he turned his eyes away in revulsion. She'd filmed the whole degrading dismemberment in the motel room, and kept the video on her phone.

The anger within him took over his body and mind. He charged at her like a raging bull, fingers wrapped around her neck and squeezed as he pushed her body backward through the air. Her phone dropped and shattered on the ground. Her fingernails dug into the flesh on his hands while her face turned red and then blue.

"You, bitch! How could you do this to me? You mutilated me? You had no right!"

Her toes barely touched the ground until he slammed her back onto the conveyor belt. She threw a kick that caught him between the legs. Seth doubled over in agony.

The girl scrambled for the exit, screaming blue murder. "Help me!"

Seth vomited all over the floor. He clutched his

groin. It was wet. His fingers were red with sticky, fresh blood. Whatever additional damage she'd inflicted down there, it didn't matter now. He was beyond repair, all the parts that made him a man destroyed in the fire. What hurt the most was that he'd chosen her. He'd chosen to save the girl from imminent death. He should have left her to die at her own devices, and her whole sinister plot to *make him a better person* would have been unraveled. But he'd done the right thing instead. Screw doing the right thing ever again!

Seth stumbled back to where the girl had dropped her phone and picked it up. He didn't want anyone to ever find that video. The shame of what had happened was unfathomable. Alone in the dark, he lay down and sobbed. The sob became a wail as the floodgates of emotion were finally unleashed. He was inconsolable, snot and tears running down his face.

CHAPTER 12

10 Years Later

The lights dimmed and a silence fell over the live studio audience. Red lights illuminated above the stage that read *"Live Recording"*. The stage was a simple setup, made to look like a cozy living room in a New York high rise apartment with ceiling to floor walls to give the illusion of sophistication and class.

Bob Charles' late night TV show was anything but sophisticated. He hosted the guests no other talk show host would dare have in front of a live studio audience, but somehow he managed to strike gold almost every time, winning seven Prime Time Emmy Awards during the show's twelve years on television.

The man himself, Bob Charles, came out onto the stage, waving and smiling. The cheesy theme music played loudly for the audience, who roared with cheers and applause. Bob was a little on the pudgy side, hair thinning on top, and had a face for radio, but everybody loved Bob, including his three ex-wives.

He sat behind a large wooden desk in the *Big Leather Chair* that had become his signature prop. The desk was infamous for other reasons; purportedly the place where many a pretty young intern had gone the extra mile for a paid job. One of them his most recent ex-wife.

It was quiet enough on the set that one of the cameramen stopped chewing his gum because it was suddenly the loudest noise in the room.

"Good evening, everyone, I'm Bob Charles, but you all know that already."

The audience applauded and Bob gestured with his hands for them to quieten down.

Bob opened a thick hardcover book that was sitting on the desk in front of him. He slipped on a pair of reading glasses and turned to the last page.

"'The shame of what had happened, I never wanted another soul to know. Alone in the dark, I lay down and sobbed. The sob became a wail as the floodgates of emotion were finally unleashed. I was inconsolable, snot and tears running down my face.'" He placed the book on the desk and removed his glasses.

"We have a special guest on our show tonight. You'll recognize him from the cover of Healthy Man magazine and his international best selling autobiographical novel *Severed: What makes a man*. I'm sure you already know who I'm talking about." Bob glanced over to the side of the stage. "Ladies and gentlemen, can I have a warm welcome for Mr. Seth Grainger?"

The audience went wild with cat calls, wolf whistles, and applause. Bob stood up and walked across the stage to greet his guest.

Seth walked out in a tailored suit, shiny black shoes, and groomed like a movie star. He was a few years older, and had really grown into his looks, all the awkward edges of his early twenties smoothed away into a fine looking man. He smiled and waved to the audience who couldn't seem to get enough of him. Bob invited Seth to sit on the three seater sofa beside his desk.

"Welcome, Seth."

"Hi, Bob. Thank you for having me."

"My pleasure, Seth."

Seth winked, startling Bob. The crowd laughed in unison.

"Right," said Bob. "No more of that, or I might start to get the wrong idea."

Another uproarious laugh from the audience.

"Sorry, Bob." Seth unbuttoned his suit jacket and crossed his legs, adopting a more relaxed pose.

"That's okay, I bring out the worst in people."

When the audience was once again silent, Bob continued.

"You know you're a hard man to pin down, Mr.

Grainger?" He turned to the crowd. "Do you folks know how much money we had to offer his agent before he would sign on the dotted line?"

Seth held a hand to his chest and feigned surprise.

"Who? Me? Oh, I'm just an ordinary guy."

"Far from it," said Bob. "Number one bestselling author in twenty seven countries, reality TV star, your own charitable foundation for abused women."

"If you put it that way." Seth laughed. "I've achieved a few things in life."

"Including being the first man in America to receive a transplant of both the twig and berries."

"Including that."

"We've all grown to love you over the years, but it's been a rocky road. At one point there you were the most hated man in America."

"No offense to you, Bob, but the media always picks a side. And at first they decided I was the bad guy."

Bob nodded in agreement.

"It seems there were a lot of people who were happy for you to live the rest of your days without a line and tackle? Feminist Magazine offered you a life-time supply of vegan hemp sanitary pads, and said, I quote, *Try this on for size*."

"Well, I've got to be honest. I didn't care what any of those people had to think. I persevered—"

Bob interjected, "And won them all over."

"Exactly," said Seth. "Well, maybe not the vegan man-haters at Feminist Magazine."

Bob chuckled.

"Something that isn't very clear to many of us," said Bob. "Is why you didn't tell the police everything up front? Why did you wait to release a tell-all autobiographical novel?"

"Everyone guilty of a crime had already been brought to justice."

"Except you."

"I'm sorry, Bob. I don't understand what you mean by that?"

"Back then there was still debate over who was responsible for giving Kerry Jones the date rape drug."

"I think there was a lot of blame in the early days, people scrambling to understand why that tragedy happened. It's been proven in a court of law that Mike Roberts, or Mikey as I used to call him, was responsible for intoxicating Ms. Jones. But I was there that night. I should have been more observant, and every day I question all the things I could have done to save that poor girl. If only I'd known what was going on in front of my very eyes."

Bob nodded his head gently and studied Seth's face for any sign of weakness, any hint or subtle giveaway that he could latch onto and run with, but Seth's steely gaze was like a mask.

Bob's eyes swept across the crowd, and he smiled.

"We have a very special someone joining Seth on the couch today. Let's bring her out."

The audience erupted into applause.

A striking blonde bombshell stepped out from the side of the stage. Seth stood up instantly and the two embraced. Everything about her was so overwhelmingly beautiful, from her toned long legs, to her movie star smile. It wasn't until the second or third glance that the baby bump was evident under her red Tom Ford dress.

The couple sat on the sofa together, holding hands. She gave him a tender kiss on the cheek and he blushed.

Bob fanned his face and looked out at the crowd.

"Welcome to the show, Amy."

Amy gave Seth's hand a squeeze. "Thank you, Bob. Lovely to be here."

"Now, I'm not the most observant guy, or so all of my ex wives tell me." The crowd laughed. "But I did notice something as you walked in."

Amy gave Seth a smile and gently rubbed her belly.

"I may have gained a few pounds since the wedding day, Bob."

"About seven and a half pounds?" said Bob.

She chuckled. "Not quite there yet. I'm due in twenty weeks."

"Congratulations. The both of you. Can I have an applause for the lucky couple?"

Hands clapped, there was whistling and chatter in the crowd.

Bob waved his hands down to hush the audience.

"So, Seth?"

"Yes, Bob."

"I guess the question everyone now has on their minds is… " Bob tilted his head and glimpsed down at his Seth's crotch. "You know."

Laughter in the audience lasted only seconds. No one wanted to miss the next few words that came out of Seth's mouth.

"I think I know what you're trying to ask, Bob." He gave the audience an over-exaggerated wink "Everything is working just as it should."

"And this will obviously be your second child."

"Yes, I have a beautiful boy, Ben who is very excited to meet the baby."

"Things okay between you and Catherine? I remember there weren't many kind words said about you in the office when our female staff reached the chapter in the book where you abandoned that poor girl outside her house."

Amy gave Seth a disapproving stare.

"Not one of my finest moments. We've made our peace. We're good friends now."

Bob hesitated and got a naughty grin on his face.

"Any thoughts of modeling for Playgirl?"

Seth's cheeks flushed red again. Before he could answer, Amy placed a hand on his chest and pushed him back against the sofa. She narrowed her gaze at the audience.

"Back off, girls, he's mine."

All three of them chuckled along with the crowd.

Seth put his hands up in the air. "I'm a lucky man, what can I say?"

Bob turned and addressed the crowd. "For those of you who have been living under a rock for the past two years, Seth has the most famous penis in the free world... that no one has ever seen."

Seth turned a shade of scarlet, and playfully hid his head behind his hands.

"I heard you got offered half a million to star in that gay porn film?"

"There was more than one offer."

"Oh, my."

The playful banter was making Seth squirm in his seat. "Can we please stop talking about my penis?"

"Your penis?"

"Now it is, and I'm eternally grateful to my donor."

Amy gave his hand a squeeze again.

Bob could see it was time to change topic. "You two met at a homeless shelter?"

They answered 'Yes' simultaneously.

"You go," said Seth, looking at his wife with adoring eyes.

"We'd both started volunteering at one of the homeless shelters in town. I saw this tall, handsome guy helping an old war veteran back into his wheelchair. He was so selfless and kind."

"Who made the first move?"

Seth chuckled. "She did."

"These days you can't get him to shut up," said Amy. "But back then, he was absolutely terrified when

I said hi. We dated for a few weeks and I couldn't understand why we hadn't done anything more than kiss. I was starting to worry he might have been gay."

Seth snorted and laughed.

"Amy was the first person I told, other than my doctor, of course. She was the one who gave me the strength to go public with my campaign to raise funds for the surgery."

"Which you raised in less than three weeks. But then the hunt for a suitable donor began, right?"

Seth nodded solemnly. "A blessing, and a tragedy at the same time. But like I said in the book, I'd rather not talk about those details out of respect to the family of the young man who made me whole again."

"Fair enough." Bob smiled. "We have time for one more question. Did the police ever find the young woman who did this to you?"

Amy and Seth both shook their heads.

"I live in constant fear that one day she might rear her ugly head again," said Seth.

Amy butted in. "I personally believe she's gone from our lives for good. Let's just get one thing straight." Amy sat forward on the edge of the seat. "Someone with psychiatric problems as serious as she had does not simply vanish into thin air. She's dead. Whether by her hand, or someone else's. Seth worries about things. It's what I love about him. But I firmly believe that bitch it six feet under."

"And the police never found out her identity?"

Seth shook his head. "Nothing. She's a ghost."

"Well, thank you again for joining us, Seth and Amy. Ladies and gentlemen, would you please give our guests a round of applause," said Bob. "We'll be back just after this quick commercial break with our weekly news roundup." He reached over and shook his guests' hands. "Thank you both for coming tonight."

"Our pleasure," said Seth.

The lights dimmed and all three left the stage. Amy nestled her head into Seth's shoulder as they walked away, the picture of a perfect loving couple. Bob stood on the edge of the stage and watched his guests leave. He couldn't put his finger on it, but there was just something about Seth that rubbed him up the wrong way, and he was a great judge of character. But everyone else seemed to worship the ground the guy walked on, so maybe this time Bob's impression was wrong. So he turned and walked toward his dressing room, moving his thoughts along to the questions he had planned for his next guest.

CHAPTER 13

Present Day

Seth was ripped from his moment of self pity on the slaughterhouse floor by a bloodcurdling scream. He looked up and saw the psycho bitch standing over him, and an axe rising in an arc above her head. Seth rolled as she brought the axe down into the concrete in the exact position where his head had been only moments before.

"Come back here, you bastard!" she screamed.

Seth scuttled to his feet and leaped over the conveyor belt. He ran for the control that was hanging from the ceiling and pushed the button to start the conveyor moving. The meat bandsaw roared to life and sparks flew in the darkness where the blade nicked the rungs. The girl was halfway over the conveyor when it started moving and she slipped onto the floor with a thud.

It took a split second for Seth to decide between running for his life and getting to the axe before she did. Their hands gripped the axe handle at the same time, starting a tug of war. She was stronger than she looked.

Seth let go one hand on the axe and threw a punch at her head. She ducked just in time and pulled the axe away from his grasp.

"You're mine now," she growled. "I'm gonna chop you up into little pieces and flush you down the toilet the way I flushed your spawn after I took to it with a knitting needle."

Her words were horrifying to Seth. He stumbled backward, eyes scanning the room for the nearest exit, or for something to defend himself against this monster.

"A bloody, tiny alien in the toilet bowl. One flush and it was gone."

Seth charged at her. She didn't have time to raise the heavy axe, so she swung it backward up at him. The heavy flat head of the axe thumped against his left chest wall, cracking several of his ribs.

Seth gasped for air and spat blood out onto the floor.

She swung the axe again. This time Seth went for her legs. His ribs crunched as he brought her down with him onto the ground. He heard a pop as her knees bent sideways from the impact. The axe flew backward through the air, far out of reach.

He crawled up her body and held her flailing

hands down by her sides. She was biting at the air like a raging zombie. Seth head butted her and an explosion of pain ripped through his skull, a headache unlike anything he'd ever experienced. Blood trickled down his forehead and into his eyes.

Her tight fist caught him in the side, right on his injured ribs. Seth rolled over in agony. The girl's foot connected with his head and everything went black for a few seconds. Seth knew if he didn't fight back that he was going to die. An inner peace was calling to him, but he knew it was a trap. He had to open his eyes and get off the ground.

Seth screamed as he sat up and grabbed her leg before her foot kicked him in the side. He tugged hard and she landed with a painful thump on her back.

He didn't hesitate again, running as fast as he could. But she was faster. Moments later she was on his back, pounding her fists against the side of his head. He spun around and tried to throw her off, but her grip was so tight she pulled out chunks of his hair. His fingers clawed into her fleshy thighs and he screamed. She bit hard on his shoulder, through his muscle down to his collarbone.

With every ounce of strength he had left, Seth threw her body to one side. She scratched the skin off his cheek as she went flying through the air, landing hard on her back on the conveyor belt, vertebrae cracking loud enough to make Seth wince. Her body arched in excruciating pain and urine soaked her panties before leaking onto the floor. She groaned loudly like an injured beast.

Seth looked on in horror. He was too far away to save her, even if he wanted to. The psycho bitch unleashed a murderous scream as the meat bandsaw sliced through her side and into her fleshy abdomen. Blood exploded in every direction. She gurgled like a dirty drain as the bandsaw screamed through its sharp, rusted teeth, grinding her spine to a fine powder.

Seth turned away, unable to watch any more.

The screams stopped as the two halves of her body slipped onto the floor with a thud. And then it was all over.

Seth ran to the girl's side.

"Oh my god, what have I done?" He held his head and rocked. "How the fuck do I explain this? Fuck. FUCK!"

He started to hyperventilate as the panic set it. The only comfort in the cold night was the warm glow from the furnaces nearby.

Suddenly, he knew what he had to do.

The room where the psycho bitch had been living was like a wild animal's nest. It had once been the supervisor's office, looking down onto the work floor. There were clothes and trash everywhere. Shards of glass on the floor, cigarette butts and syringes had gathered in layers of filth over the years since the slaughterhouse had closed down.

The meat bandsaw was still roaring, and in the background was the sound of the furnaces crackling. The wall was covered in polaroid pictures of Seth, Mikey, and several other guys he'd never met, a collage of people and places, covered in red marker pen scrawl.

Was I her first victim?

Seth looked at his pants, which were soaked down the front with blood. He was beginning to feel light-headed and woozy again. He saw a small device sitting on the ground beside the bed that looked like a harmonica. Seth picked it up and pressed the button on top. When he spoke, his voice came out modulated like a robot, the same as the one he heard speaking to him on the phone.

He lay down on the girl's bed, which was nothing more than a couple of old feather down blankets on top of a rat bitten, thin camping mattress. It stank of mold and urine, but was soft and hugged his tired, weary bones. He decided he would close his eyes, but only for a second.

Seth woke himself with a jolt.

How long have I been asleep?

It was still dark outside. The slaughterhouse was

completely silent and pitch black. The generators had run out of gas.

Seth picked his heavy head off the ground and pushed himself back onto his feet.

I think I'm dying.

His heart was bounding so fast in his chest, every beat pounding against his broken ribs, causing sharp stabbing pains that made him moan and wheeze like a squeaky toy.

He pulled the phone out of his pocket and switched on the flashlight. The darkness seemed to swallow the light, which only illuminated a few feet around him.

Seth stumbled down the rickety metal stairs that threatened to fall apart with every step he took, groaning against his weight. He turned and crossed the processing floor to get to the furnaces, afraid of what he might find.

There was a faint odor of burnt pork that he tried to ignore as he entered the smoking room. His eyes scanned the dark corners and he held the flashlight on the phone up high enough to illuminate every shadow, terrified the psycho had somehow managed to survive, that she might launch herself at him from a secret hiding place and finish what she had started.

He knew his fears were unfounded. She wasn't coming back. She was a monster, but there was nothing supernatural about her. It took another hour to scrape every bit of ash out of the furnace and rinse it down the drain on the main killing floor.

The sun was just beginning to rise and shine light through the broken windows when Seth stumbled back to the processing floor and lay on the ground. He had no energy left, his body was shaking, and his head throbbed. He pulled out his phone — the battery was almost dead — and dialed *911*.

THE END

A NOTE FROM WARREN

Well, if you've made it this far then I hope you thoroughly enjoyed the depravity that was *Severed*. If you didn't enjoy the book and still read to the end, then I would seriously recommend you seek mental health advice because you're one sick puppy — like all those weirdos out there who watched *A Serbian Film*.

I had a huge amount of fun writing this story, dreaming up a plot that would be any man's worst nightmare. There were times when I stood in front of the mirror naked at night before having a shower and thought "Sheesh, am I being too tough on poor Seth." What do you think? I'd love to hear your thoughts on Severed.

Please leave a review to show your appreciation. Reviews lead to sales, and sales inspire me to write more stories. I'm sure you can appreciate that this results in a win for both of us. For your ease I've included a link below (I'm helpful like that).

If you spot any glaring errors or typos, I would appreciate that feedback, too. I'm still not sure that I counted correctly how many pills Seth took. Even with the best editors, mistakes seem to find a way into the published product, little shits that they are!

ABOUT THE AUTHOR

The eldest of the brothers. Warren was born in England, where he spent his childhood terrorising his younger brothers on his parents' livestock farm. The family cashed up and emigrated to the United States when he was a teenager. After high school, he worked in the IT sector until the crash in the early 2000's when he decided to head back to University to study English and French, with the dream of becoming an author.

www.warrenbarns.com